I Am Beloved

In the Footsteps of Saint John

POOJA CHILUKURI

Healing River Press

I AM BELOVED
In the Footsteps of Saint John

Copyright © 2022 by Healing River Press and Pooja Chilukuri

Paperback   ISBN: 978-1-732-5858-7-4
Digital   ISBN: 978-1-732-5858-6-7

Library of Congress Control Number: 2021924396

Published in the United States of America

This is a work of fiction based on the four gospels—*Mathew, Mark, Luke,* and *John*—and does not make any claims of adhering to scriptural accuracy. The Bible References Section at the end of the book contains all the NIV Bible references under the terms of use listed by the International Bible Society.

The map of Palestine in Jesus' time is used under the Creative Commons License.

This is a work of fiction. Names, characters, places, events, locales, and incidents are either the products of the author's imagination or used in a fictitious manner. Any resemblance to actual persons, living or dead, or actual events is purely coincidental. This work does not intend to hurt the sentiments of any religion, sect, denomination, community, or individual.

For more information, visit www.poojachilukuri.com

For any queries, permission requests, or special pricing on bulk book orders, contact Pooja Chilukuri at pooja.chilukuri@gmail.com

To you, the beloved.

Foreword

Pooja Chilukuri, sister in Christ, who has a loving, genuine heart for Christ and His message of hope and redemption through personal relationship, has crafted a step back in time through the life and eyes of an apostle Jesus dearly loved. As we read the Holy Scriptures, we are often left to fill in the blanks of the settings, time periods, and the cultural breath of the people. Writing this fictional account of John allows a reader to imagine what was and could've been.

Pooja is a gifted storyteller and a woman of strong conviction. Anything that she writes, whether it is to promote positive health and nutrition choices, her memoir, or her poetry, revolves around Christ as the center. It has been an honor and blessing to know Pooja personally. She is truly a remarkable woman and a supportive friend. When in Pooja's presence, the quiet and peacefulness of faith covers the atmosphere, allowing a calmness that can only be described as tapping into the Holy Spirit in the everyday. Pooja's words will also do that to you. They'll transform you and allow you to travel back in time to a place we often wish we could be as believers, by the side of Jesus.

The challenge is to read the Biblical account of the life of Jesus, then turn to Pooja's novel. I pray you see the words crafted here, and they come alive for you. Thank you, Pooja, for going after words that matter and writing this fictional account of the life of John. I am sure it will bless many as it has me.

Dr. Jennifer Lowry, Ed. D.
Author and Owner of
Monarch Educational Services

"I will call them My people, who were not My people,
And her beloved, who was not beloved."
"And it shall come to pass in the place where it was said to them,
'You are not My people,'
There they shall be called sons of the living God."
Romans 9:25-26

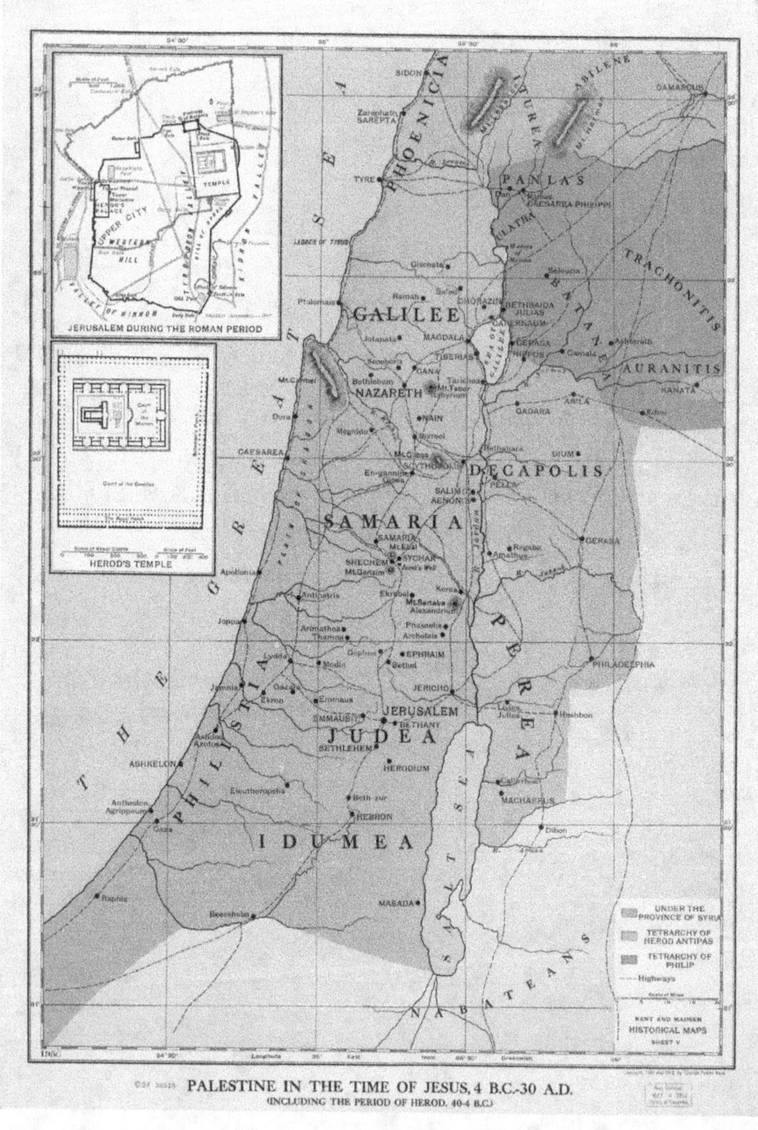

JERUSALEM DURING THE ROMAN PERIOD
HEROD'S TEMPLE
PALESTINE IN THE TIME OF JESUS, 4 B.C.-30 A.D.
(INCLUDING THE PERIOD OF HEROD, 40-4 B.C.)

1

Mount Calvary, Outside Jerusalem, 33 AD

My stomach churned as I stood on that mountain of death. Sweat dripped down the back of my neck. The crisp spring air offered no respite. It was on this skull-shaped mound, outside the walls of the holy city, that the blood of my people flowed like a river. Thousands of Jews had been crucified on this hill at the whim of our Roman rulers. Some suffered for raising their voices; others were sentenced to death for bearing the sword against their oppressors. The Romans took delight in publicly displaying the horrors of these punishments. Those who witnessed these crucifixions trembled as they recounted them. Fortunately, I had been spared the horror of such a spectacle.

Until that day when I stood witness to the killing of an innocent man.

I watched as death closed in on him. His breath got heavier with each passing moment. A thin red stream trickled from the wooden beam on which the Roman soldiers pinned his body driving heavy iron nails through his wrists and feet. His agonizing scream resounded in my ears. The sweat mixed with drops of blood gathered as jewels upon the makeshift crown of thorns that adorned his forehead with the written charge posted above it: *this is Jesus, King of the Jews*. His face was disfigured, eyes were swollen shut. His bones peered through pieces of flesh that hung from his back. A chill ran down my spine. The same fate awaited us- the ones whom Jesus had chosen as his disciples.

The Sanhedrin, the city council, accused Jesus. "He blasphemes against our God." They convinced the Roman governor, Pontius Pilate, that Jesus had instigated us to bear arms against Rome. "He opposes Caesar!"

The irony must have escaped them. Jesus taught us many things but being skilled in using the sword was not one of them. Even at the time of his arrest, Jesus stood by his words — all who live by the sword will die by it.

Since Jesus refused to resist his captors, it left us with no choice but to run and hide. However, a stubborn, unseen force compelled me to follow Jesus throughout his trial and conviction. Perhaps it was the umbilical cord between Jesus and me. Then again, it might have been the hope that Jesus somehow would bring down fire from heaven, any moment, and destroy those who plotted his death.

I had reason to hope.

Jesus was no ordinary teacher. He made the mute speak, the lame walk, and the blind see. Have you ever seen a dead man raised to life? I have. Jesus did this more than once. It would take countless scrolls to list all the miracles he performed. Surely, he was the Messiah, the one who would deliver us from our political oppressors!

But our nation's leaders were divided on this matter. Some believed that Jesus was delusional, a lawbreaker leading the masses astray. Others said, "Can a lawbreaker do the miracles he is doing if God were not with him?"

On that day, while some beat their breasts in grief, many mocked him. "If you are the son of God, save yourself by coming down from the cross."

My heart raced. At once I recalled Jesus' words: "Do you know I can ask my Father (God) to put at my disposal over twelve legions of angels?"

But there were no angels. No miracles. Not even a word from Jesus.

The chief priest and elders shouted. "He saved others. Why can't he save himself?" Those who passed by mocked him. "If you are the son of God, come down from the cross!"

Their words pierced my soul. It was not the first time in three years since I trusted Jesus as my rabbi, my teacher, and mentor, that the dark clouds of doubt engulfed my heart, but it was the first time that I felt utterly devoid of hope. Our priests and religious leaders found Jesus lacking when measured against our laws. Why didn't he contest any of the charges that the rulers brought against him? Did he mislead us? How could he forsake us now?

Maybe Jesus was not the Messiah. My heart sank.

His silence was deafening.

And when he spoke, at last, his words pierced my heart. "John, take care of Mother." His mother, Mary, was clinging to me. I tightened my grip on her limp body. She had been with me from the moment of Jesus' trial before Pilate.

He spoke once again, this time addressing his mother. "Woman, from now on, John is your son." Mary remained motionless; her gaze fixed upon Jesus. I heard him gasp as he strove to raise his body to draw a breath. His struggles, however, were the least of his concern—we were foremost on his mind.

I broke down and wept. The one I loved was dying. I buried my hands in my face. My knees gave way. I had been there before, thirteen years ago.

His name was Abel.

2

Jerusalem, 20 AD

It was a Passover to remember.

I accompanied my family along with a caravan of pilgrims to Jerusalem, the holy city, to celebrate this spring feast. As we approached the city gates, my heart skipped a beat. The temple of our God loomed large on the horizon. Its marble and gold sanctuary dazzled like a diamond in the noonday sun. The pillars and columns that girded the courtyard disappeared into the clouds. We trudged along a gradual ascent to the temple mount from the gates of the city. I groaned. The blisters on my feet were oozing blood. I had been eager to show off my new sandals—a treasured birthday gift from my mother. A boy only turns thirteen once—the day he becomes a man, as custom dictates. I could not wait to celebrate my first Passover as a 'man'.

This festival was central to our traditions. Any Jew, young or old, could recount the tale of our prophet, Moses, calling down plagues upon the land of Egypt where our forefathers served as slaves. The final plague was the angel of death striking every firstborn in Egypt, sparing every Jewish home that had the blood of a lamb smeared on its doorpost. To honor the memory of this deliverance, each year we visited the temple, sprinkled the blood of a blameless, firstborn, male lamb upon the altar of thanksgiving, and partook of its flesh.

Purchasing the lamb had been a formidable task. The best of the herd had sold out fast. My father had emptied his purse to buy the ceremonial animal. He charged me with its care, transferring the responsibility from my older brother James, who had been lording it over me for the past four years. Guarding the lamb until the moment of its slaughter was no ordinary endeavor. Any injury would render it a useless offering. I was determined to make my father proud. I barely slept the entire week as I watched over Abel, for that was the name that came to mind the moment I laid my eyes upon him. He followed me around all day; at night I slept with him close by side. I made sure he remained unharmed.

I held Abel in a firm grasp as we approached the temple gate. He lay still, his head buried in my chest. As we entered the temple grounds, we passed by the animal sellers and money exchangers, along with the Gentiles (non-Jews) who were permitted assembly in the outer courts. The inner courtyard was bursting at the seams with Jewish pilgrims. The bleating of lambs filled the air. They wriggled to let loose from their captors -the priests who had the hallowed charge of slitting their throat. A shadow crossed my heart. As I beheld the blood of all the other lambs being poured into offering bowls, a giant pit appeared in my stomach. Traitor, murderer! I felt a lump rise in my throat. Should I let Abel loose?

But alas, my heart grew cold. I could neither risk the wrath of my father, who strove to follow every letter of our laws nor dishonor the memory of our ancestors. Most of all, I feared offending the God of our forefathers.

And so, when it was our turn, I surrendered Abel to the priest. Abel squirmed. Ba-aa-aa. He was perplexed and panicked at having to relinquish the safety of my embrace. I stood tall with my head held high, even as my hands trembled.

The priest slit Abel's throat, spilled his blood in a bowl and stripped the skin of Abel's back, and pierced him on a pole where he was to remain until the night of the feast.

In a tryst with irony, Abel was the namesake of an individual recorded in our sacred texts—one who was betrayed and murdered by his brother, Cain. Cain was a prisoner of jealousy, but I was bound by an age-old institution. I hoped Abel would forgive me.

At once, everything went dark.

When I regained consciousness, the whiff of a spiced perfume that my mother had used to revive me greeted me. She was hovering over me in tears. My fainting had caused her much alarm.

I hid my face in my hand; I was no man.

That was the first and last time I handled the Passover lamb.

At the Passover meal the next night, not wanting to draw any more attention to myself, I nibbled on Abel's meat. That night, as I lay tossing and turning in bed, my stomach gave up its contents. Alas, that did not lessen the load of my heart.

Mother was right. It was best to refrain from these rituals of blood.

My father was unable to contain his disappointment. "You need to be a man like your brother." My mother rushed to my defense. "His time will come."

My time did come; however, redemption did not come easy.

3

The Northern Jewish Province of Galilee, Bethsaida, 23 AD

I grew up to be a fine young man, according to my father. No, I never lived up to his expectations regarding temple rituals; I found other means to make him proud, a discovery I chanced upon. One day, he noticed me catching fish with my bare hands. His eyes sparkled when I scooped them out of the waters—three in a row. I had stumbled upon a golden opportunity to drink from the cup of his favor. I resolved to be the best fisherman. In time, I became adept at running our family business—a thriving fishing enterprise in the small town of Bethsaida, on the northeastern shores of the Sea of Galilee, also known as the great Lake of Tiberias.

The Sea of Galilee was my home. It was a wellspring of life. Cradled in the rift valley of the Jordan river, which connected the Jewish provinces of Galilee in the North to Judea in the South, the rich soil and the freshwater attracted both fishermen and farmers alike; clusters of villages sprung up along its shores. Fueled by underwater springs, the Jordan river, and mountain streams, the sea abounded in living creatures. I would spend long hours scouring its bounty for fish, basking in the kisses of the spray from its crashing waves which carried my cares away. The sea was my companion—each current, every ripple whispered in my ears. My fellow fishermen grew to rely upon me to alert them of its moods, especially its fury, which arose with little warning. I never failed them. My father's chest puffed up. He gave me the title, 'master of the sea.'

At our house, James was the shining star. My father made his desires known—a man must honor the God of our forefathers, carry forth the legacy of our ancestors, conduct his family affairs with righteousness, and bring pride to his nation. However, the greater burden of these obligations fell on the firstborn, James, who did not disappoint. He tended to all our traditions and rituals with great care and even brought home a beautiful bride that satisfied Mother's heart. She finally stopped pestering me to become a family man. Being the younger sibling had its advantages, after all. Besides, not that my heart never beat for a girl, but that it beat louder for my nation.

Since the age of five, frequent trips across the Sea, to the synagogue in the town of Capernaum on its north-western shore, were not an option. Father desired we be trained in the book of our law, the Torah, and learn from the best. The synagogue, made of white limestone blocks, and set at a height above the rest of the town, housed a renowned rabbinical school within it. Holy men, the rabbis who belonged to the religious sect of the Pharisees, were our teachers. They occupied prominent seats in the synagogue, presiding over the prayers and the study of our scriptures. Their attire boasted of their piety. They strapped a tiny locket containing scripture to their foreheads, and long tassels hung freely from the edge of their cloaks. Most Jewish men wore garments with these tassels, which reminded them of the laws given by God to our prophet Moses. The length of the tassel was regarded as a measure of holiness. Our rabbis flaunted theirs.

The rabbis upheld every letter of every law laid down by our God and imprinted them upon our hearts and minds, all six hundred and thirteen of them. James could recite them all. I could never catch up with him, perhaps because during the lessons, my mind would drift to the tales of prophets and kings like King David. While yet a young shepherd boy, David defeated the giant Goliath—a Gentile who blasphemed God and challenged our nation—with a mere slingshot and a stone.

These accounts of the triumphs of our ancestors over those who rose to subjugate us fired me up unlike the laws, which raised more questions than answers, like why did Abel have to die? One hopes to outgrow their wounds, but not when one must relive it. Every Passover brought Abel to mind. I dared not opt-out of the celebration to obey my father—a man must not bring disgrace to his family, or his nation. He permitted me to wait in the outer courts of the temple as they fulfilled their blood rituals. I consented to take part in all other related festivities. However, I refrained from the meat of the sacrificial animal. At first, father had hesitated and said, "One must be careful not to displease the Lord!" But mother had been quick to quote from our scriptures, the song of King David: "The Lord pities those who look to him; he remembers we are dust." Without a doubt, I inherited my zeal for our prophets and kings from her.

I cherish the memories of my mother reciting the tales of the triumph of our ancestors. I recall being awestruck as she shared of our prophet Moses flying at the giant Og, king of Bashan, and striking him with only a large stick. This battle fought on Mount Hermon, the highest peak visible from the sea, was the last step before the next milestone of victory—the entry into the land promised to our forefathers by God. Under their commander Joshua, they established an independent nation whose glory reached its zenith under King David and his son Solomon. This land, flowing with milk and honey as God promised, stretched from Mount Hermon in the north to the Dead Sea in the south across the provinces of Galilee, Samaria, and Judea. This was to be our haven where we flourished under God, but alas, an immense shadow fell upon our paradise.

We had a turbulent history of kings. Some chose not to follow God's ways. The kingdom was divided, followed by its inevitable and ultimate defeat—bondage to foreign rulers for five hundred years and counting.

As we struggled to preserve our identity under the Roman rulers, our temple in Jerusalem, in the southern province of Judea, stood as the beacon of hope, the pride of our nation. It brought harmony across the various religious and social strata of the Jewish populations scattered throughout the Roman empire. Those who revolted against the breach of its sanctity paid for it with blood. Tales of Jewish massacre within the temple courts, and the exaltation of the Gentile symbols, such as the Roman eagle, and the Greek columns and structures within the temple premises, made my heart burn. What were my people to do?

Thousands took up the sword against Rome. They were crucified or beheaded. This only fueled our resolve for freedom. Many revolutionaries joined hands to form a band against the political establishment; these were known as the Zealots. One from this group, Simon Iscariot, also known as Judas, had a hold on James; James had many secret meetings with him, which was a bone of contention between us. Trouble followed Judas. However, James argued that taking up the sword was the only way to reclaim our power. I disagreed. Mother had planted the seed in me: "The battle belongs to the Lord."

I pinned my hopes on the words of the prophet Isaiah:

> "The Spirit of the Sovereign Lord is on me,
>   because the Lord has anointed me
>   to proclaim good news to the poor.
> He has sent me to bind up the brokenhearted,
>   to proclaim freedom for the captives
>   and release from darkness for the prisoners,
> to proclaim the year of the Lord's favor
>   and the day of vengeance of our God,
>
> They will rebuild the ancient ruins
>   and restore the places long devastated;
> they will renew the ruined cities
>   that have been devastated for generations."

His words filled me with the assurance that God would avenge our humiliation and our oppression. Surely, He would send us one as great as Moses to establish us as His chosen people, cleansed of foreign defilement, restoring our lost glory under his appointed rulers once again.

I waited and waited….

And waited…

It had been seven centuries since Isaiah foretold the coming of the anointed one.

Where was he?

4

With time, unlike some, I refused to get accustomed to my nation's enslavement. I was tethered to the hope of one as great as Moses, which fanned the flames of my restlessness. My father's advice for peaceable coexistence–pay your taxes, stay away from the Zealots, the Roman centurions, and Herod's men–fell on deaf ears. If only I could silence the stirring within!

The lush regions around the Sea of Galilee drew a host of settlers from across the Roman world—both Greeks and Romans; pious Jews did not intermingle with these Gentiles. I resented the emergence of the Greek cities, Tiberias on the western shore, being the chief of them. Its grand architecture was a memorial of forced Jewish sweat, including both the tax from our toils, and forced labor for the massive building projects. It was the capital city in the Galilean province ruled by the cruelest tyrant, Herod Antipas; Antipas renamed the sea, the Lake of Tiberias, after the Roman emperor Tiberius, yet another erosion of our identity. Having these outsiders defile the land of my forefathers was bad enough. Must they invade my sea too?

The foreign invasion of the sea was also detrimental to our business. The rise in the number of fishing boats, which competed for its waters, pierced its tranquility. This raised an alarm for the fish; they refused to bite during the day, driving us to cast our nets at night or combine them with other fishermen. We hired some as helpers and partnered with two others—the brothers Andrew and Simon.

Andrew and Simon, our childhood companions, were natives of Bethsaida. Their family owned the largest fishing boat in town, and we had the strongest nets. Andrew's foresight prompted us into a timely partnership; that year we had to sell some of our boats to keep up with the monstrosity of increasing taxation.

Andrew, Simon, James, and I were a mixed lot. On the sea, we labored as brothers, taking turns casting our nets both night and day. Off the sea, we had as much in common as not. Andrew devoted himself to the study of our laws and the prophets, and took charge of our enterprise; Simon, when not occupied with cleaning the boats, loitered in the streets with the Zealots, learning to use the sword from them lending his voice to their chant 'blood for blood'. Simon did not care to commit our laws to memory. He also did not share in my aspiration of the Messiah convinced that many deceivers have come in his name. I could not argue with that. From time to time, a 'messiah' would emerge, leading people astray, preying on their deepest longing and faith. The last one led people into the wilderness of the Judean desert, where they were crushed by the Roman army. To Simon, yearning for a messiah was like chasing after the wind. He did not need rescuing. He slept with his sword by his side. Besides, Simon was preoccupied with mouths to feed—a wife, children, a mother, and a mother-in-law as well.

Andrew was Simon's strength, following the death of their father. Andrew never married; I never asked why. He was our rock. There was never a wrinkle upon his brow. He was four years older than James and Simon, and eight years older than me. When my hope for an independent nation would grow dim, Andrew would assure me with these words: the one whom the prophets have foretold will reveal himself any day. No wonder a slice of my heart left with Andrew when he and Simon moved their family to Capernaum, across the sea. I missed not being able to knock on his door when I tired of James' admonishment: "Be a doer, not a dreamer; take up the sword or take on a family."

Andrew had proposed the move and with good reason. The Sea was churning out catfish, which was an abomination to devout Jews but welcomed by the Greek patrons in Tiberias, south of Capernaum. As much as I shunned those outsiders, I cared for our survival; I complied with Andrew's request to engage with the Gentile customers. He remained unbiased towards them, unlike most radical Galileans. Perhaps, a result of his frequent travels to the southern, more Hellenized, province of Judea.

Magdala was yet another town on the western shores of the sea where we hauled our fish frequently for pickling and preserving. Bethsaida was under the tetrarch Philip, whereas Capernaum Tiberias and Magdala belonged to the territory of Herod Antipas. Traveling to Antipas' district came at a cost—the border tax. The tax collectors stationed in Capernaum would charge us sometimes two or three times over. Our pleas fell on deaf ears. That was not the worst of it; one of them was our own, Matthew. We considered him a dog or pariah (outcast), for he betrayed our nation by rendering his service to foreign masters. When these tax collectors responded to our patient negotiations with contempt, Andrew decided to have the last word.

Andrew advised Peter to set up residence in Capernaum, putting an end to our dilemma. We would fish together and then part ways. Andrew and Peter would sell a portion of our catch on the western shores of the Sea of Galilee while James and I took care of the villages on its eastern shores. It was a relief from having to contend with the tax collectors. We made the best team, not just as fishermen. I could not imagine my life without my brothers. Little did I know then that I would outlive them all by a good number of years, and not because I was the youngest.

5

The Southern Jewish Province of Judea, Bethany, East of River
Jordan, 29AD

"I am not the Messiah."

I pushed through the crowd to get a glimpse of him. His voice, like thunder, emanated from a lean frame wrapped in long hair, an unkempt beard, and clothing made of camel hair with a leather belt tightly girded around the waist. He was from the lineage of priests. However, he was least likely to be found in the temple courts; he roamed the wilderness of Judea instead, surviving on wild locusts and honey alone. He spewed out judgment against the evils of the religious and political establishment, much like a prophet.

His message was as fierce as his appearance: "Repent, for the kingdom of God is at hand."

Although some held him as delusional, others felt threatened by the growing number of his disciples whom he immersed in the river Jordan, befitting his nickname—the baptizer. This immersion ritual of baptism was akin to our purification rituals, especially before we entered the hallowed places in the temple to prepare for worship. However, the baptizer claimed that his baptism prepared people for the holiness of God's righteous kingdom, which the Messiah would establish. This perplexed the religious authorities. If anyone was going to have the last word on the Messiah, it should be them. They were threatened by the baptizer for they alone wielded authority over the purification rituals. Thus, the temple authorities in Jerusalem sent a delegate of priests and Pharisees to confront John—yes, the baptizer was my namesake.

"Are you the messiah?" they asked.

"No," he replied, "I am only here to prepare the way for him."

"Are you Elijah?"

"No!" John's voice rang loud and clear.

Elijah was one of our mighty prophets who never tasted death. Legend dictates that he ascended to heaven in a chariot of fire.

The Pharisees shouted at him. "You are neither a prophet nor the Messiah, then by what authority do you baptize?"

The baptizer laughed. "You worry about this purification by water? The ax is at the root; He who baptizes by fire is amongst you already! Its flames shall consume the old order of things."

The temple delegate shook their heads and left muttering curses under their breath. "Why bother with the words of a madman?"

But my heart skipped a beat. I clutched Andrew's arm. Was the Messiah here already? The baptizer seemed to think so, and Andrew believed him.

When Andrew had brought news of the baptizer, I needed no persuasion; We prepared to journey from Capernaum to the region of Bethany, in Judea, to meet him. James had stayed back to take care of business while we dragged Simon with us.

John the baptizer preached about the imminent kingdom of God and performed the rituals of water purification preparing those who were ready for change—ready to be unshackled from the old ways of political bondage and religious corruption, for our high priest's office, appointed by Rome, was subservient to it.

Every fiber of my being longed to jump into the waters of the Jordan. I was ready to surrender to the lordship of God's chosen servant who would restore our nation to its righteous ways and its lost glory. I was ready for his kingdom.

I must have had that look on my face—the look of a hungry dog eager for crumbs from the master's table. Andrew was quick to observe. "Not today, John," he said, pointing to the enormous crowd that surrounded the baptizer. "The water will be here tomorrow and so will the baptizer." He pointed to the nearby hills where we had pitched our tent. "We must hurry before night falls." At once, I was aware of the desert chill. I hoped Simon had a fire going.

Upon returning to the tent, I was relieved to find that Simon had arranged for both a fire and a warm meal. While Andrew recounted to Simon the details of our eventful day, I plopped myself on a blanket by the fire. The travels of the last two days and the excitement by the riverside caught up with me. My body ached, unable to move, but my heart jumped with anticipation. As I basked in the comfort of the crackling flames that leaped high, I wondered what the baptizer had meant when he said, "He will baptize by fire." Would he bring down fire from heaven and drive away the Romans as Moses defeated the Pharaoh in Egypt?

The next day, I hurried to the river at the crack of dawn. I could hear Andrew's gentle snores and Simon had started cooking breakfast, but I could not wait. I had to get to John before the crowds did. Andrew had been baptized already during his last visit; It was my turn.

A pleasant surprise awaited me. A thin wall of people hid John from my view. But I could hear him from a distance. His voice had a ring to it. "Behold, he is the one I spoke of!"

My heart leaped out of my chest. Who was John talking about? Surely not the Messiah!

I strained to catch a glimpse as I dashed to the river. I saw a man emerge from the water. Long, wet hair and a thick beard hid his face. Before I could get to the riverbank, he walked away.

Later, as I stood before John in the waters of baptism, I asked him how he could be so certain that the one who was there a few minutes prior was the Messiah. He said, "I saw God's Spirit descend on him like a dove and heard a voice from heaven saying, 'This is my son.' He is God's chosen and we need not wait for another."

I rushed back to my tent to bear the good news to my brothers—"I have found the one of whom the baptizer speaks!" Andrew believed me. Simon was still unsure. Andrew accompanied me back to the river.

That is when I saw him again. I would not have known it was him if John had not once again pointed to him and said, "Behold the lamb of God, who takes away the sins of the world! He is the one for whom I must prepare the way."

At last, the one who could remove the sins of corruption and oppression from our nation! I resolved not to lose him again. Andrew and I ran after him, following at a distance. He must have known. He turned around and a broad grin lit up his face. "What do you want?" His voice was like gently falling rain. He was at least as old as Andrew. His attire was as our rabbis but without the long tassels. His kind eyes twinkled, lighting up his rugged, weather-beaten face. For a moment, I faltered. Could he be the one? At the least, he seemed to be a teacher. Andrew was quick to speak up. "Teacher, we want to see where you live."

We spent the afternoon with him. We learned that the teacher was from the town of Nazareth, south of Capernaum, in Galilee. He was seldom in his hometown and frequently traveled across both Galilee and Judea. He was a most gracious host. As we ate lunch together, he taught us many things in our scrolls concerning the Messiah, much of which made sense to Andrew, for he was well-versed in the Torah.

I could barely concentrate on the teacher's words. I was consumed with the question—is he the one? I dared not ask him. Neither did he say, "I am the Messiah." My excitement gave way to caution. If he was the Messiah, why did he need to be baptized by John? Did he not have the authority to baptize or recruit disciples for his kingdom's cause? How could the Messiah be like one of us? Many such questions led me spiraling down into the pit of doubt. But for Andrew's confidence, I would have remained there. Andrew could never be wrong.

The following day, a skeptical, albeit curious Simon accompanied us to the teacher's tent. We spent yet another afternoon with him. Simon seemed to take to him, although he doubted his authority as the chosen leader for our nation.

Messiah or not, I desired to linger awhile with the teacher. Every time he spoke, something in me stirred. He informed us he was preparing to go into the wilderness of Judea for an undetermined time of fasting and prayer. It saddened me, not knowing how I would find him again.

I need not have worried about that.

He found me.

6

Bethsaida, Sea of Galilee, 30 AD

I barely shut my eyes the previous night. The fish had gotten adept at hiding. We fished all night and returned empty-handed. Andrew seemed to think that the smaller fish were escaping from the gaps in our nets where there were tears. James and I spent our morning mending the nets so we could try our luck once more that night. The noon-day sun and the cool sea breeze almost lulled me to sleep when a familiar voice snapped me out of my trance.

"Follow me!"

My jaw dropped. It was the teacher!

He was not alone. Andrew and Simon were with him. At once, I let go of my net and followed them. I had not expected to see him again. It had been a few months since our last meeting. Also, what was he doing in my hometown?

Andrew read my mind. "The teacher is staying with us this week and preparing to bring the message of God's kingdom to our synagogue, this Sabbath!"

I did my best to contain the flutter in my stomach. At last, the moment I had been waiting for! I was eager to do as he asked—to follow him.

The first place he led us was the pier where we had docked our boats. He pointed to them and signaled Simon and Andrew. "Pull them out and cast your nets." Simon shook his head. "We have been up all night and caught nothing. There is even a lesser chance during the day!"

Jesus smiled and said, "Cast your net on the right side."

Simon glanced at Andrew, unsure of what to do, but Andrew had pushed the boats out already. He nodded. Simon turned to the teacher and said, "We will do as you say."

Before the teacher could motion to James and me, I was already in the water pushing our boat. James followed.

In no time, our boats were full, and our nets broke. Was this a coincidence? Simon certainly did not think so. He fell on his knees before the teacher and wept. "Surely, you are the holy one from God; depart from me my lord for I am not worthy." But the teacher stooped down to lift Simon, embraced him, and said, "Simon, do not be afraid. From this day forth, you will catch not only fish but men. You shall be known as the rock (Cephas or Peter)."

I was amused. I would have never considered Simon a rock, fire, or wind perhaps, but not a steady piece of stone. But I was not one to question the teacher's wisdom. From that day onwards, the name Peter stuck with Simon, and eventually, he became an important and immovable pillar for our cause.

James and I went back home to pack some of our belongings, mostly clothes, as the teacher instructed us to travel light. We were headed to Capernaum and from there to wherever the teacher led us, not knowing when we would return.

Father had witnessed the miraculous catch of fish. His chest puffed with pride as he bid us farewell. "Bring honor to your nation, go in peace. We have enough hired hands here to take care of business till you return."

Mother was far from anxious. She pronounced her blessings on us as well. "Serve well my children so that when the Messiah establishes his kingdom, you will be one on his right, the other on his left." It was hard for James because his wife was with child, but once we set sail for Capernaum, all he could think of were the adventures ahead.

And so, we took leave of home. Another young man, Philip, from Bethsaida, whom the teacher had chosen, accompanied us.

We were men on a mission, steeped in the magic of youth where no mountain is too high, no valley too low, and the horizon ours to conquer. We resolved to follow the teacher, hoping that he would restore the lost glory of our nation. We did not know how he planned to do it, but we trusted he would teach us his ways and prepare us for victory over our foreign rulers.

That Sabbath as he taught in the synagogue at Capernaum, he expounded on prophecies concerning the Messiah from our scriptures and assured us of the fulfillment of God's promises at the appointed time. The rabbis were in awe. "No one spoke like this man!"

The day after the Sabbath, the teacher instructed us to travel to the town of Cana, south of Capernaum, in Galilee. I assumed we would start our training, but the teacher was in no hurry. He surprised us with this announcement: "We have a wedding to attend."

7

Cana, Galilee, 30 AD

When we arrived at the wedding in Cana, we encountered a boisterous crowd of cheering and dancing guests who had too much to drink. We had traveled a full day south and west of Capernaum by foot. I was grateful for the stone bench in the courtyard, where I relieved my stiff back upon arrival.

I noticed six large stone jars in the corner containing water. The servants rushed to fill their jugs. As they poured the water on my feet, a custom that not only cleanses the dust from our travels but also eases our weariness, I felt a surge of energy. The teacher's relatives and his mother extended a warm welcome to us.

I was ready to join the celebration.

My first look at Mary, his mother, sufficed to determine where the teacher inherited his gentle but firm demeanor, kind lips, and determined brows. Her eyes spoke of a sleepless night and an eventful day. She and the bride's parents left no stone unturned in ensuring a grand wedding, one that the whole town ought to remember.

They would have never guessed how that would come about.

Despite their best efforts to prepare for the wedding party, the wine ran out. The guests had shown no restraint, but that would never pass as an excuse for the inability to meet their needs. It was too late to buy wine from the sellers, but Mary was not one to concede defeat. She pointed to the teacher and commanded the servants. "Do as he tells you."

The teacher gave his mother a look that said, 'not now, mother', but Mary was a determined woman on a mission to save her relatives from disgrace.

The teacher motioned to the servants and said, "Draw all the wine you need from those stone jars." He pointed to the stone jars that contained water—the same that we had used earlier to cleanse our feet. I could not resist the urge to correct the teacher. "Those jars contain water."

I noticed his mother attempting to subdue her grin. She instructed the servants once more, pointing to the teacher saying, "Do as he tells you."

They did. The servants returned, astonished and excited. "Who is this man who bends the laws of nature?"

My curiosity aroused, I ran to the pitcher. I rushed to the water jars and stifled my scream. A dark sparkling liquid greeted me. Could it be wine? I dipped my fingers inside and drew some out to touch my tongue.

It was wine. The best kind.

It was a sign from heaven! I could not subdue my excitement. What more evidence did I need that the one as great as Moses was here? Moses had turned water into blood as a warning to Pharaoh to release our forefathers from their chains. The teacher had transformed ordinary water into priceless wine; transforming the fate of our nation was next.

I rushed off to alert the others. "Teacher is the Messiah." But my brothers were not sure. "The wine may have already been there, the servants may have made some mistake!" Even Andrew set off to cross-examine the servants.

But I was an eyewitness.

My hope grew wings that day.

This was the first miracle that the teacher did in public, but his instructions perplexed me. "See to it you tell no one, for my time has not yet come."

But this did not keep me from pondering the matter with my brothers, who were yet unsure. I was excited and contemplated the teacher's next move, which turned out to be fulfilling a teary-eyed request from his mother. "Son," she said, "we have not seen you in over a year; when will you come home?"

And so, we accompanied the teacher's mother back to their hometown, Nazareth, a two-hour journey south of Cana.

A rude awakening awaited us there.

Nazareth, Galilee, the Following Day

At the teacher's house, I could not help but notice all the impeccable details carved into beautiful wooden furniture—benches, tables, chairs, shelves and stands all placed in an orderly manner. His mother noticed my admiration and declared proudly, "Jesus is skilled at his craft." That is when I learned his name, a detail that, up to this point, had gotten lost in my excitement. I learned that day that he was a carpenter by trade and the oldest among four brothers (James, Simon, Joses, and Judah) and three sisters, Salome, Mary, and Anna.

That night, as I lay in bed, I could not help but wonder that something was amiss. My brothers would have been all over me if they had not seen me for a year. Jesus' brothers, however, seemed cold. James, younger than Jesus by a year, hardly spoke to him beyond a greeting. Perhaps his brothers resented Jesus' absence, as that meant taking on more than their share of household duties. And then it occurred to me—Jesus' brothers did not believe he was anyone special.

They were not the only skeptics. The next day, being Sabbath, we visited their synagogue. My heart warmed up within me as Jesus read from the scroll of the prophet Isaiah a passage that I was all too familiar with:

"The Spirit of the Lord is on me. He has anointed me. He has sent me to announce freedom for prisoners."

What he said next made me giddy with joy. "This scripture is fulfilled as you hear me speak." This could mean only one thing. He was God's chosen deliverer for us.

His bold declaration received a mixed response. Some said, "Is this not the carpenter's son? How dare he make this outrageous claim!" Others said, "He speaks with such authority!"

The leaders of the synagogue ran us out of town and forced us into a corner; it was the edge of a cliff from which they planned to push Jesus in their fury but failed even as we walked away peaceably from their midst.

Jesus had been right in his judgment earlier—a prophet is not honored in his hometown. A pit appeared in my stomach; I longed to return home to the sea.

Jesus must have sensed my yearning. He instructed us to leave for Bethsaida the next day. But alas, Bethsaida would prove just as disappointing, with a hint of a silver lining. No one attempted to murder us there.

Although Jesus did many miracles in my hometown, healing all their sick, blind, mute, and lame, the people refused to open their hearts to him—they had mouths to feed, families to tend to. Besides, if the Romans did not interfere with their everyday lives, why care for God's kingdom at all? There was no need to break the monotony of a peaceful fishing village.

And so, we set sail for Capernaum, where a different challenge awaited us.

8

Capernaum, Galilee, 30 AD

The Rabbis at the synagogue in Capernaum shook their heads. "Can anything good come out of Nazareth? The Messiah will come out of Bethlehem." They quoted our prophet Micah: "But you, Bethlehem, though you are small among the clans of Judah, out of you will come one who will be ruler over our nation Israel."

Andrew and I were in Capernaum, engaged in debate with our teachers at the synagogue. My heart sank as they pointed to the scriptures. I could not refute our prophets, but Andrew was quick to assure me. "Teacher was born in Bethlehem; you know He is the one."

I heaved a sigh of relief. The Pharisees were not convinced. "What proof do you have?"

Andrew was not one to be deterred. "Come and see for yourself!"

The Pharisees followed us back to his and Simon's house, where we lodged along with Jesus. The house was bursting at the seams that day with long lines extending beyond the courtyard. Enormous crowds had gathered for news of the signs and wonders which Jesus had performed earlier, both in Capernaum and surrounding towns, spread far and wide.

In Judea, the disciples of John the baptizer had also proclaimed the miracles of Jesus, and his fame piqued the curiosity of the temple authorities who sent a delegate of Pharisees to Capernaum to investigate. Amidst the crowd, I noticed another unwelcome visitor standing afar in the courtyard—the tax collector, Matthew.

As Jesus taught us about the kingdom of God, the people were dumbfounded. "No one has thus enlightened us. How can he speak with such authority?"

Some were hesitant to embrace him, for the teachers of our law and the high priest at the temple had yet to grant Jesus the seal of their approval. The temple delegate murmured amongst themselves. "These unlearned masses sway easily."

While Jesus was yet teaching, the roof over his head opened and a cot dropped at his feet, causing a great commotion amidst the crowd. A paralyzed man lay on that bed. Four of his companions, frantic to approach Jesus amidst the crowd, had carried his bed and lowered it through a hole which they carved in the roof.

Jesus reached down and placed his right hand on the man's heart. "Your sins are forgiven, son."

A deafening silence permeated the room. Only God could absolve sins. Surely, the Messiah could not exercise the authority of our God! Not even Moses nor any other prophets dared to do so.

Knowing my thoughts, Jesus turned to me and said, "Do you suppose this man is crippled by disease or by fear of judgment? Which is the better assurance, your sins are forgiven or be healed?"

The man jumped from his bed, and fell at Jesus' feet, weeping. All who witnessed this were stunned. But the Pharisees were furious. Jesus had committed the inconceivable in the eyes of the law—blasphemy. No man could forgive sins, and none could be absolved without ritualistic cleansing. That day onward, they sought his arrest at an opportune time. Apprehending him then could have ignited riots. Because the paralyzed man was healed, the crowd was fired up in Jesus' favor.

The people refused to let go of Jesus. I was getting impatient, hungry, and concerned about Jesus. He had not had anything to eat or drink since the break of day; It was almost afternoon, but Jesus looked refreshed. As he would often say to us, his food was to do the work of one who sent him.

One of those who sought his blessings that day was Simon's Zealot friend Judas Iscariot. Jesus blessed him and agreed to let him join our mission as he requested. A shadow crossed my heart. Judas had the reputation of a fickle-minded instigator. Trouble followed him. I wanted freedom as much as he did, though not by the sword, but by the hand of God's power demonstrated through his chosen one like Moses.

For the rest of the afternoon, Jesus blessed and healed all who were sick, and taught with compassion all those who were hungry to learn from him.

As the people went on their way, Matthew slipped away as well; he did not escape Jesus' notice.

Jesus motioned to us. "Come, follow me."

Where could we be going at this hour, when it was time to wind down our day? But Jesus was just getting started.

We followed Jesus to the tax collector's booth, the same one that we encountered often on our travels back and forth across the sea. To my dismay, he approached Matthew saying, "Follow me!" I was unable to contain my disappointment—not this traitor! Devout men did not associate with such. Besides, these tax collectors had caused us enough trouble already, extorting more than their fair share from us. Fortunately, Simon had stayed back to help Andrew fix the roof, else he might have had a fit. Andrew would not have cared since he never took things to heart.

Jesus sensed my disappointment. I recall his gentle chiding to this day: "Just as the sun shines alike on all, so is the kingdom of God for everyone."

You can imagine the look on Simon's face when we walked home with Matthew. "What is he doing here?" Simon bellowed.

Matthew broke out in a sweat. His voice cracked. "Please accept my invitation for dinner."

Later that night, as we dined at Matthew's house, some Pharisees came to know about it. They pointed to Jesus and said, "How can a man from God eat with such sinners?"

Jesus' eyes softened. "The healthy do not need a physician, but the sick need healing." The Pharisees shook their heads and left.

They were not the only ones who disapproved. My chest tightened. Joining with those who befriended our enemies was not the way to cleanse our nation. Simon also stood in a corner, downcast. Jesus went up to him and placed his hand on Simon's shoulder.

Simon asked, "how many times must I forgive him, teacher?"

"Seventy-times seven, Simon."

I glanced over at Simon. He did not respond. Forgiveness is a long road.

9

Jerusalem, Spring 31 AD
Morning

Jesus appointed us the twelve as his disciples—Andrew, Simon, James, and I, along with Philip, Nathaniel, Matthew, and Judas Iscariot. Jesus also chose another James, son of Alphaeus, Judas, son of James, and Simon the Zealot. We accompanied him to Jerusalem for our first Passover celebration. We arrived a week ahead of the Passover sacrifice, planning to purchase our lamb at the temple.

A great multitude accompanied us because Jesus' reputation had reached far and wide. The previous few months had been hectic—we had been with him as he tended to the lame, the blind, the deaf, the mute, and those oppressed in their minds. He instructed us to proclaim the kingdom of God to the towns and villages, which we were eager to carry out.

I paused for breath on the Mount of Olives on our way to the temple, beholding its grandeur; a shadow crossed my heart. The rays of the sun from the cloudless sky beat down on the temple mound, and my eyes fell upon the citadel in its northwestern corner. It was the Antonia fortress constructed by our previous ruler, Herod—a bloodthirsty wretch. Our then ruler, Antipas, his son, was no better.

As we proceeded towards the temple, my steps grew heavy. The arcade and other grand structures built in the temple grounds by Herod were a painful reminder of the desecration of the house of our Lord. Herod did not serve our God, only himself. He poured Jewish blood within the temple courts, further eroding its sanctity. Even our priests, who were set apart for serving God, fell prey to corruption and intimidation by these rulers. When Herod put up the sign of the Roman Eagle at the temple gates, two of our scholars took it down. They paid for it with their life while the priests stood back and watched them being burned to death with Herod gloating over their defeat. Our rabbis in Capernaum had recounted these tales and more.

Rome controlled the high priest's office, and Herod appointed many of the priests. As a symbol of resignation, the priests handed their garments, the symbol of their authority, to the Roman soldiers who stored them in the towers of Antonia and permitted their use during the feasts and festivals.

Many Jews, especially in Jerusalem, learned to co-exist alongside the garrison of Roman soldiers stationed at the Antonia Fortress. At least six hundred men on any day, and many more during our festivals. Their patrolling the perimeter of the temple pricked my heart. The Roman governor of Judea, Pontius Pilate, lived west of the holy city at Caesarea Philippi. He relied heavily upon the Roman army to uphold peace in the city. The previous rebellion by Zealots had ended in three thousand crucifixions and a pile of corpses in the temple. I shuddered. The sword never ended well for us. I trusted Jesus had a plan, a plan to deliver us not by the sword but by fire, as our prophet Moses had done for our forefathers.

B a a … B a a a … B a a a a a …

The bleating of lambs filled the air, pounding on my ears and snapping me out of my musings. At once, I felt my knees become weak. With the adventures of the past few months, Abel's memory had dwindled; However, what my mind had erased, my body remembered; I faltered. Fortunately, Andrew grasped my hand in time.

I hoped Jesus and the other disciples had not noticed. Whatever reservations I had about the Passover, I kept to myself. Only James, Andrew, and Simon, now called Peter, knew of my quandary.

As we entered the temple courts, we had to squeeze through the crowds.

The cooing of doves, the grunting of cattle, the bleating of sheep and goats, and the clinking of coins on the tables of the money changers greeted us. The din of hagglers, and those who stood to profit from them, made the temple seem like the fish market of the large cities. Could Jesus restore it to its splendor from the days of King Solomon, who first established it?

Jesus made a whip out of cords and drove out the animal sellers and the money changers, overturning their tables. "How dare you turn my Father's house into a den of thieves?"

The animal sellers and money changers were extorting large profits from weary pilgrims. Those who sojourned from afar purchased their offerings at the temple for convenience. Besides, they could not risk the animal or bird getting injured on the journey, rendering them a useless sacrifice. These worshippers who traveled from non-Jewish provinces were at the mercy of the money changers to exchange their coins, which bore Caesar's inscription, for the Shekel used in the mandatory temple tax.

Jesus continued to cleanse the temple of those who exploited the worshippers. "Get these out of here! My Father's house is a house of prayer for all people!"

I was astonished. Jesus, who was as gentle as a lamb, roared like a lion that day.

My anticipation grew. Was he going to tear down the Herodian structures as well?

The temple leaders shook their fists. "Who gave you the authority to tear down the temple market?"

Jesus replied, "Tear down this temple and I will build it again in three days."

All who heard Jesus shook their heads. How could he tear down and rebuild a structure that took forty-six years to build? We did not understand what he meant, not until much later.

The religious leaders accused him of conspiring to destroy God's holy dwelling, and we presumed he would destroy the foreign structures and replace them with those that honored our God and our forefathers. Some Zealots, like Judas Iscariot, felt assured that Jesus would avenge the blood of our forefathers that cried out in the temple courts by waging a war in its grounds—a misconception that would cost us dearly.

Jesus taught and healed many at the temple that day. The religious authorities shook their heads in displeasure. "How dare he! Without our permission?"

But the crowds were seized with amazement. "No one taught us like this man! Can anyone perform these signs and miracles if God were not with him?"

From that moment, many followed us, fueling the frustration of the temple authorities who dared not apprehend Jesus, fearing an uprising.

Evening

We had pitched our tent at the foot of the Mount of Olives, an hour's walk from the temple. There was a grove about a stone's throw away from our tent, the garden of Gethsemane. Jesus would often retire there to pray.

After the excitement at the temple, we returned to our tent hungry and tired.

Jesus gathered his prayer shawl. "Eat and rest; do not wait for me."

Devout men used the prayer shawl as a head covering as a mark of respect for our God. I marveled at how it never left Jesus' side, no matter where we roamed. As I watched Jesus disappear into the olive grove, I could not help but wonder — why didn't he stay back at the temple to pray in God's holy dwelling place? I, myself, had never offered prayers to God except through priests during rituals and sacrifices at mandated feasts and festivals. I made a mental note to ask Jesus about it.

Night

The long day turned into an even longer night. Deep darkness and a heavy desert springtime chill had set in. I threw some dry branches into the fire, which was on its way out. Each one had retired to his tent. James, Simon, and I were sharing our tent with Jesus. The others, including Andrew, had pitched their tents near us. I could hear their gentle snores. One of us would take turns during the night to keep watch and keep the fire going; I volunteered for that first watch.

The excitement of the day had caught up with me, and I dozed by the comfort of the fire when the noise of the crunching of dried twigs startled me. I was wide awake. In a flash, Peter was beside me with his sword drawn. "Who is it?" he asked. "Maybe a wild mountain goat or a fox," I said. But I was wrong.

A well-built figure of medium height, his face covered with a long shawl, advanced towards us. Peter clutched his sword. It was a man and no ordinary one. As he uncovered his face, we realized he was one of them—the great Sanhedrin—the highest religious and legal delegate of seventy-one members, typically Pharisees. Was he here to apprehend us? Peter drew his sword.

"I come in peace!" the man stepped back. "I seek to learn from the teacher."

Before Peter and I could advance towards him, we heard a familiar voice. "Nicodemus!" Jesus had returned, and he now addressed the man who stood trembling before us, taken aback by the sword.

"Teacher, I know you are a prophet sent by God, for no one can do the things you do nor teach the way you teach." Nicodemus fell at his feet.

Jesus stooped down to lift him, warmed up his meal, and offered to share some with Nicodemus. As they reclined by the fire, Peter and I retired to our tent.

Peter suggested we keep watch. He did not trust the authorities. I coaxed him to go to bed while I kept guard.

Nicodemus had snuck out into the dark and tracked us down. He dared not be seen with Jesus during the day, for fear of being cast out by the temple ruling council who had already branded Jesus as a troublemaker and blasphemer. Nicodemus thought otherwise. He recognized that Jesus' authority exceeded that of a typical rabbi.

Nicodemus spoke with childlike innocence. "Teacher, when will you establish the kingdom of God?"

"It is here, Nicodemus. Do you not perceive it? It is like the wind which blows, which you cannot see, but you can recognize its effects."

"How can I recognize it, teacher?"

"You must be born again?"

"How can we enter our mother's womb a second time?"

"Flesh gives rise to flesh," explained Jesus, "but it takes awakening by God's spirit to discern his kingdom."

Jesus' gentle tones floated through the silence of the night and made their way into my semi-sleep trance. Surely, Jesus was going to bring judgment upon the Roman rulers and establish God's kingdom soon, and God would send his spirit upon our people so they might believe in him as their deliverer. On that note of comfort, I drifted off to sleep. I did not stir until Jesus entered the tent; He pulled my blanket over my feet and laid his shawl on top of it. It was then that I realized I had been shivering. I lay awake for a while, reflecting. This Passover had felt different. For once, the memory of Abel had not dominated. Also, there had been too much excitement at the temple with the confrontation with the authorities. No one had dared to stand up to them as Jesus did. Their fury towards him made my flesh crawl.

The next day, I was hesitant to return to the temple for the Passover sacrifice; fortunately, Jesus instructed me to stay back and make dinner preparations. During the Passover meal, he noticed I passed up the flesh of the animal offered; I searched his face for raised eyebrows or signs of disappointment. I was greeted by kind eyes and a warm smile.

Something stirred in me; Messiah or not, I did not know, but of this I was sure—Jesus was my brother.

10

Summer, 31 AD
Judea

"They are seeking the teacher's life; it is best if you leave by night." The one who warned us was Lazarus.

Lazarus and his sisters, Mary and Martha, were Jesus' friends who brought much cheer and comfort to all of us disciples. Their hearts and their home in the small town of Bethany, east of Jerusalem, remained forever open to us.

Following the Passover celebrations, we had received word that the baptizer, John, had been taken captive by Herod Antipas' men. That tyrant sought to crush John's fiery tongue, for he called out Herod on his adulterous misdeeds. Distressed by his arrest, John's followers requested us to tarry awhile in Judea with them. So, we spent a few weeks at Bethany enjoying the hospitality of Lazarus and his sisters as we assisted Jesus in ministering to the disciples of John.

During that time, we made both friends and enemies. Jesus had made his way into the hearts of the Judean villages surrounding Bethany, inciting both anger and jealousy of the temple leaders who feared losing their grip over the masses who followed "yet another prophet who could lead them astray." They were still seething in rage at Jesus, who had neither consulted with them nor cowered under their threats, as he rid the temple of those who harassed the worshippers.

Jesus remained calm. "It is not my time, nonetheless, prepare to head back to Galilee by way of Samaria."

James and I dashed off to prepare for our journey home. The news of the imminent threat, though unwelcome, could not have come at a better time. We had received word that James had become a father. I had barely recovered from the excitement of becoming an uncle, else I might have resisted Jesus' instruction for traveling through Samaria, a province sharing its northern border with Galilee and its southern boundary with Judea.

The Samaritans were a hostile lot. We, pious Jews, shunned them, a resolution bred from generations of animosity between us. Even though they claimed a Jewish heritage, we deemed them as Gentiles, for their forefathers took foreign wives; our laws strictly mandated otherwise. Our rejection did not deter them from imitating our temple worship by building a holy altar on mount Gerizim. They also had their lineage of priests that served in this temple, which we did not deem sacred. However, the one thing we Jews shared with them was the Roman occupation of our land.

But this was not the time for me to begrudge the Samaritans. Traveling through the Samaritan towns could shorten our travels by as much as a whole day. I could not wait to get home and greet the recent addition to our family—a baby girl.

Sychar in Samaria

As we traveled through the Samaritan province, the noon-day sun beat down on us without mercy. We were hungry and weary from our travels, needing a respite.

At last, we arrived in the town of Sychar, where our forefather Jacob had dug a well. I could not contain my disappointment when I set my eyes on it. It certainly was not as spectacular as it appeared in the tales that mother told of Jacob and his twelve sons from whom the twelve tribes that comprised our nation Israel descended. This well was a gift from Jacob to his favorite son, Joseph. I had imagined it as a grand structure, only to find a narrow hole in the ground through which a man of my stature could squeeze through with some difficulty.

There was one thing that fascinated me about the well. Its depth. Layers of limestone were chiseled and removed to access the water hidden in the bosom of the earth.

It was then that I realized I was lightheaded from thirst. I was not the only one.

Jesus had found a spot on a rock near the well and had taken off his sandals. That was our signal to break for lunch. Andrew and the others went into the nearby towns to buy food.

I peeped inside the well.

"It's no use, John, we have nothing to draw with, but maybe she can help," Jesus said, pointing to a woman who advanced towards the well with hurried steps.

She nearly dropped the pitcher when she noticed us. I perceived the well was a gathering place for the women folk earlier in the cool of the day, not at the hour when the sun was at its peak of fury.

The woman took a few steps back. Her head covering was drawn over half her face, revealing her thin lips curled downward in a frown. She was not expecting to run into anyone, especially men.

"Can you give us something to drink?" Jesus asked.

Jesus' Galilean accent likely alerted her. "Do you not know, sir, that Jews do not eat or drink from the same dish as Samaritans?"

By this time, I was so overcome by thirst that I was ready to snatch her pitcher and draw from the well myself, but Jesus patiently answered her. "If you knew who asked of you, you would ask him, and he could give you the water of life, springing forth from within you."

His words were a riddle to me.

"Go call your husband," Jesus instructed the woman.

"I have none."

"You are right in saying so. You have had five husbands and the one you now live with has not taken you as a wife."

The woman stepped back. Then she lifted her veil and fixed her eyes on Jesus.

"I perceive you are a holy man!" "Tell me," she continued with fervor, "who is right, the Jews who believe God dwells in Jerusalem or we who believe that Mount Gerizim is God's holy sanctuary?"

By this time, she had set aside all her inhibitions and was hungry to engage the one whom she sensed was a prophet of God. I had set aside my thirst as well and was all ears. Surely, Jesus would take a stand for our holy city, Jerusalem!

His reply baffled me. "A time is coming when the temple of God will be neither Jerusalem nor Mount Gerizim. God seeks those who worship in spirit and truth."

The woman raised her eyebrows. "Will not the Messiah restore the lost glory of our temple and re-establish it?" "When he comes," she continued, "he will explain all things to us!"

I refrained from rebuking her. The Messiah would come for us, not for them.

"I am he," replied Jesus.

I was astounded. A surge of energy shot through my bones. This was the first time I heard Jesus make this much-awaited claim. Then a dark cloud descended.

How could the Messiah choose to reveal his identity to a Samaritan woman ahead of us disciples who had been with him this whole time in anticipation? We followed him as our teacher, but we always knew there was more to him though no one dared ask, especially since he bid us many a time not to proclaim his miracles far and wide saying, "It is not my time, yet."

I choked on the lump that rose in my throat. The woman, however, was beside herself with excitement. She dropped her pitcher, her face uncovered, she ran back to her village shouting and waving her hands. "Come see the one who knows everything I ever did! Is he the Messiah?"

By this time, I had used her pitcher to quench my thirst, and my strength had returned. Jesus was energized as well. A host of villagers, led by the woman, flocked to Jesus, marveling at "the prophet from Galilee"; many Samaritans believed in Jesus as the Messiah and invited all of us to lodge with them for two more days. However, James and I were eager to get home. Jesus, who never failed to heed our needs, bid James, Judas, Peter, and me to travel ahead of him and the others. Andrew, who was adept at handling the crowds, volunteered to stay with Jesus.

Sleep evaded me that night. I was excited to be the first among the disciples to have heard Jesus declare he was the Messiah. I resented that Jesus regarded the Samaritan villagers worthy of him, but I basked in the hope that someday we would be free of those Romans now that the one as great as Moses was here.

My thoughts then shifted to Andrew. His responsibilities of managing our daily food and lodging and handling the crowds that followed us around kept him on his toes. He and I barely had time to speak to each other. James, Peter, and I spent most of our time ministering alongside Jesus and learning from him. Andrew and I had grown apart in some ways, especially since he spent more time with Matthew, who assisted him, and it pricked my heart each time I saw them together. How I missed casting nets in the sea with Andrew, Peter, and James! I could not wait to be home.

11

Bethsaida, Summer, 31 AD

As we journeyed from the plains of Samaria towards the hills of Galilee to the foothills of Mount Carmel, I drew a deep breath. My heart burst forth in song. It was on this mountain that our mighty prophet, Elijah, called down fire from heaven on our wicked ruler Ahab and his false prophets who served their deity, Baal. I was never tired of the stories of Moses or Elijah.

And now one greater than Elijah was here.

Jesus had revealed Himself to the woman at Jacob's well as the Messiah; it was a matter of time that we would stride into freedom and victory over our oppressors. I set aside my resentment of him having revealed himself to a Samaritan ahead of us who followed him faithfully. I was bursting with joy, but not everyone shared in it.

Judas had been tight-lipped for the entire journey, save for this singular outburst. "The Messiah did not come for those Samaritans!' But Judas' sour spirit failed to dampen my hope.

Peter and James agreed with Judas, which appeased him. I wish I had paid closer attention to the wound that festered in Judas that day—one that would lead to much agony for all of us.

As we crossed the region of Mount Carmel and headed towards upper Galilee, a sense of relief overcame me, for unbeknownst to me, underneath all my excitement, I had been bearing a load—a sense of foreboding. Those who sought Jesus' life would be sure to thirst for our lives as well. I shuddered. It was good that we would be home soon.

At last, we glimpsed the Sea of Galilee, as beautiful as ever, glowing like a bride under the light from the moon rising upon its waters. James and I parted ways with Judas and Peter, who were also eager to be with their families. We hitched rides on separate fishing boats and headed home.

The Sea and I had much to catch up on. Her waves frolicked around our boat, eager to tell me the tales of all I had missed in the last few months, but they would have to wait till the next day. Night had set in, and I was eager to partake of mother's lentil stew and hold a newborn infant.

At home, everything seemed perfect, every object in its place just as I remembered, and yet much had changed. Father seemed to have expanded around the waist, and mother had gained a few extra wrinkles. They were in high spirits, more than I ever recalled. Becoming grandparents had served them well. As for James, he transfixed his gaze on the treasure nestled in his bosom. That was the first and only time I saw my brother cry. A baby had put a chink in his 'manly' armor. As he handed her to me, I wondered how any mortal could be so lovely. I clasped my hands around her fist that day, not knowing that her arms would one day be my strength. We gave her a name that was in keeping with the delight she gifted us with—Aliza, meaning joy.

As I retired to bed that night, my body was sore, but my heart was at ease. I was safe at home. The past few months had been laden with travel, adventures, wonders, and excitement. However, the recent conflict with the leaders and the threat to our lives cast a shadow on it all. All I wanted was the comfort of my home, my family, and the sea.

But alas, ships are for the waters, not the safety of the harbor.

After two days at home, I was ready to spring into action. The comfort of home was a temporary haven, perhaps an illusion. Zeal for my nation's deliverance had consumed me. More so now that the Messiah was here.

As I drifted off to sleep that night, a swirling mix of thoughts danced around in my head: thoughts of being at sea with my brothers, prancing around the slopes of the Golan Heights, mother telling us stories on the Sabbath, father's admonishment over matters of the law, little Aliza untouched by guile, and then the flash of a Roman sword.

I bolted upright on my bed.

We were slaves. Slaves may dream of only one thing. Freedom.

The next day, our house was buzzing with excitement. Preparations for hosting the Messiah were underway. Mother saw to it. "We must be sure to be of excellent service."

Mother also did not waver in her appeal to him, "Lord, when you establish your kingdom, grant my sons a seat at your right and left hand!"

Jesus answered her with compassion. "You do not know what you ask for; can you drink from the cup assigned to me?"

"Yes!" we answered in our folly, oblivious to how bitter it would prove to be.

12

Capernaum, 31 AD

As Jesus' popularity soared, so did our troubles. Multitudes followed us everywhere, through all the towns and villages of Galilee and Judea, and the Greek-occupied regions across the river Jordan. The sick often pushed through the masses to touch Jesus with eager expectation of healing. Jesus did not disappoint, touching Jews and Greeks alike. Among them were the lepers, the lame, the mute, the blind, and those oppressed by demon spirits. One such individual was Mary of Magdala, whom Jesus delivered from seven demons. She, along with a host of women, ministered alongside us.

Word of Jesus' miracles spread like wildfire. It became impossible to shake off the crowds. The chief priest and temple authorities from Jerusalem sent several spies to Capernaum, who mingled with the crowds, seeking ways by which they might gather evidence against Jesus to convict him. They would have preferred putting him away but feared an uprising for his hold on the masses had exceeded that of John the baptizer.

The rabbis at the synagogue in Capernaum muttered amongst themselves. "Could Jesus work miracles if God were not with him?"

The delegate of Pharisees from Jerusalem persuaded them otherwise. "He leads masses astray. The crowds are ignorant of the law and easily deceived."

Their most grievous charge against Jesus was "blasphemer" because he addressed God as father and encouraged us to do the same. This was a serious charge, punishable by death, for no one dared approach God so carelessly, especially without ritualistic cleansing offered by our priests. I must admit this teaching intrigued me, and I approached it with some trepidation myself.

Contrary to our laws, Jesus performed some of his healings on the Sabbath day, infuriating our leaders. Jesus confronted them. "Sabbath was set aside for Man's benefit; Man was not created to serve the Sabbath. If your sheep or goat falls in a pit, will you wait until Sabbath is over to rescue it?"

Jesus' bold claim outraged the leaders further, for they were the keepers of our laws and enforced obedience to its every letter.

The leaders in Jerusalem, who had sold their soul to Rome, cared nothing for our laws. Pride had darkened their hearts. "How dare this small-town rabbi (teacher) challenge our authority!"

Praises and adulation from the masses caused our chest to puff up; however, the threat from our leaders and their contempt kept us in check and on the edge. When some teachers from the synagogue in Capernaum came seeking Jesus' favor, we were skeptical.

"The centurion, Flavius Marcus, requests your favor, Rabbi," they beseeched Jesus. "His servant, whom he loves as a son, is sick and dying!"

Did the Roman centurion not have access to the best physicians in the empire? Why did he not bring his servant to us himself? Why send word through our teachers from the synagogue? Was it a trap?

It turned out that the others shared my apprehension. None of us welcomed the Roman soldiers, much less the centurions in charge of them. I cannot recount all the horrors of the readiness with which they used their swords, not sparing women or children. When James was ten years old, the Roman centurion had called him and his friend, Levi, 'Jewish rats'. Levi had taken offense. All that James recalled was the flash of a sword and lots of blood, Levi's blood. Although James never spoke of Levi over the years, I suspected that his memory lurked as a demon in the shadows.

He was reluctant to follow Jesus to the centurion's house. So were the rest of my brothers. They went off to sharpen their swords.

~

"Blood leads to blood, James; put your sword away." Andrew's voice was stern.

His instructions fell on deaf ears. James, his face flushed, continued to sharpen his sword.

Andrew covered his face with his hands. "A sword or two or ten is no match for their hundred."

"And Teacher does not need us to defend him," I added. "He can call down fire when he wants!"

"What is he waiting for?" Judas chimed in. I noticed the glint of the tips of his daggers carelessly concealed inside his cloak.

His eye caught mine as he shoved them in deeper. "It is coming up on a year this Passover since we left home to follow him; no fire, no plagues, he speaks of loving our enemies. Would the Messiah betray our nation?"

For once, I could not disagree with Judas. Jesus' teaching, "pray for those who persecute you," puzzled me. Moses, in his anger at injustice towards our enslaved Jewish forefathers, had killed an Egyptian in cold blood. Was Jesus truly as Moses? A cloud crossed my heart. Matthew was quick to dispel it.

"The scriptures point to him being the Messiah."

Working closely with Andrew had rubbed off on Matthew. Peter could care less. His dislike for Matthew had not waned. He clutched his sword. "Better safe than dead," he said, looking past Matthew at Andrew.

"The centurion helped build our synagogue, Peter." Andrew attempted to persuade him and us, but to no avail.

And so it went, as we headed to meet the centurion, everyone held on to their swords—all except Andrew, Matthew, and I.

As we left the room where we had gathered in Peter and Andrew's house, I caught a whiff of ether, the most expensive kind. It came from Judas. No one else noticed. I shook my head in disgust. He oversaw our money bag. I had no doubt he was dipping into it.

We cast aside all our apprehensions when we set our eyes on Flavius Marcus. He rode alone, coming to greet us halfway. Flavius Marcus knelt before Jesus. He surrendered his sword and his shield at Jesus' feet. "I do not deserve you to come under my roof. The teachers of the synagogue may have neglected to let you know, but all I need from you is to speak the words, and my servant will be healed." He pointed to the Roman eagle on his shield. "I, too, am a man of authority commanding scores of men under me. If I say come, they come; if I say go, they go! I know your power exceeds mine."

"I have yet to find such great faith in all of Galilee and Judea," said Jesus. "Go in peace; your servant is healed."

The centurion bowed with gratitude and took off on his horse. The teachers of the synagogue followed him. They confirmed the servant received healing at the exact moment that Jesus commanded it.

Upon witnessing this miracle, some respected members of the temple council, who had traveled from Jerusalem to monitor our activities, also trusted Jesus as the Messiah. Chief among them was Joseph of Arimathea, who would befriend us in our hour of great need.

As for Flavius Marcus, his faithful service to Rome helped him move through the ranks. A few months later, he was stationed at the Antonia fortress northwest of the temple mount to serve the Roman procurator Pontius Pilate, governor of the region of Judea.

I heaved a sigh of relief; the shedding of blood had been averted. Some of the disciples did not share in my consolation. They were disappointed, and despite the evidence of the miracles, they continued to question if Jesus truly was as Moses?

It would take a storm to dispel our doubts.

~

The crowds that followed us that day as we made our way to greet the centurion held on to Jesus. He had compassion on them, regarding them as sheep without a shepherd. They, too, never tired of listening to him like he never tired of teaching them. They welcomed his parables, a change from the solemn recitation of scriptures at the synagogue. Some had never even set foot inside one. In his zeal to minister to the crowds, he refused food and water. By the time it was evening, he was faint with exhaustion, so were we. He instructed us to row across the lake to the other side to get away from the crowds.

"What is the matter?" Peter asked. My face always gave away my feelings.

"The sea forbids us riding upon its waters, just yet." I pointed to the currents in the sea.

I sensed a strong wind had disturbed its waters somewhere from the eastern shores. We were likely headed into a storm.

Peter looked up at the cloudless skies. "We have two pairs of oars and a sail; we can cross to the other side in no time. Do you want to be buried under these crowds?"

I was in no mood to argue with him. I was eager for a warm meal and a bed. Besides, a big boat, not the wind, may have disturbed the waters.

It was dusk by the time we set sail. The others took turns at the oars; my body was stiff from standing all day while tending to the crowds. It was smooth sailing for the first hour. We had rowed halfway across eastwards, when a giant wave crashed over our boat, catapulting us into a rip current. A furious wind descended upon us from the Golan Heights and battered its sails. The sea raged and roared. I should have trusted its warning. Jesus was in a deep sleep. We despaired as we struggled to keep the boat from turning over. We screamed in unison. "Lord, do you not care if we drown?"

Jesus stood up, turned, and faced the waves. He raised his hands and commanded them. "Be still!"

At once, the wind died down. The sea was like an infant on its mother's breast. Its waters caressed our boat, which drifted upon it, its sails ripped to shreds. We all sat down, stunned.

Jesus broke the silence. "Did you think I was going to let you drown?"

No one looked him in the eye nor answered him. We marveled at what we had witnessed.

Who was he to whom nature yielded her glory?

There was no question in our hearts that he was a man of authority, as the centurion had acknowledged. By the evidence of the signs and miracles Jesus performed, we knew he was the Messiah. But that night, I felt there was more to Jesus.

As I observed his kind eyes deeply set under his wrinkled brow, exuding quiet confidence, a whisper crossed my heart. Could this be the face of God?

Then my father's voice echoed in my head. "You cannot see God and live!"

Since that day, we disciples, never asked each other "who is he?" I relinquished my title to Jesus that day. He was the *master of the sea.*

My hope was restored. Could there be another Messiah who could do greater works than Jesus? Casting out my doubts, I set my heart to learn from Jesus and follow where he led. Perhaps there was an appointed time where he would gather an army and lead us to Rome. He commanded the wind and the waves; raining fire from heaven was a matter of time.

Eventually, Jesus did rain fire from heaven. It was not on the armies of Rome. It was on us.

13

Galilee, Mount Hermon, 32 AD

The majestic, snow-capped peaks of Mount Hermon, towering over the northern edge of the Golan Heights, took my breath away. I was no stranger to the region of Golan, but that day, as Peter, James, and I followed Jesus up the rugged slopes of Mount Hermon, my heart raced. I was treading where Moses may have once trod. The mountain was sacred to us and rich in legends. From its lofty ridges, our forefathers, under the leadership of Moses, caught their first glimpse of the land God promised them. In my excitement, I failed to notice how far we had climbed. I could see the Sea of Galilee in the distance and touch the clouds. We lost sight of Jesus.

His voice broke through the clouds. "Let us rest here."

I clutched my cloak a little tighter and shivered. Peter lit a fire. Why had Jesus led us there? James read my mind. He glanced at me and shrugged.

Jesus often retired to the mountains to commune with God; Jesus had taught us to pray, but communion with God was a privilege reserved for priests or prophets—a legacy from our ancestors. When Moses received the commandments from God on Mount Sinai, our forefathers were terrified when they beheld the glow on Moses' face, which nearly blinded them. I recalled the lesson which the Pharisees at our synagogue emphasized from the scrolls of Deuteronomy where Moses recorded the plea of our forefathers: "Let us not hear again the voice of the Lord our God or see this great fire anymore, lest we die."

And in the same scrolls, Moses recorded God's pledge to our people to raise a prophet like Moses to lead us: "I will raise up for them a prophet like you from among their brothers. And I will put my words in his mouth, and he shall speak to them all that I command him."

At last, such a prophet, who commanded even the winds and the seas, was here! My heart skipped a beat, wondering what marvel awaited us. We had barely warmed up by the fire when a flash, like lightning, pierced the thick clouds that descended on the mountain.

It was Jesus.

He was transfigured. His clothes and face shone like the sun.

And then we saw them—Moses and the prophet Elijah.

I was beside myself with excitement and overcome by wonder. My body became like a feather. Peter fell at Jesus' feet. "Lord, permit us to build a shelter here, one for you, one for Moses, and one for Elijah!"

However, just then, a thick, bright cloud enveloped us. We fell to the ground, covering our faces with our cloaks. A gentle and firm voice pierced the cloud. "This is my son, whom I love; with him, I am well pleased. Listen to him!"

I do not know how long we laid on the ground, awestruck and fearful. Jesus touched us and assured us. "Do not be afraid."

We looked up. Moses and Elijah had vanished. I smiled at Peter. There was no need to build tents for three. One would suffice, for he, who was greater than Moses and Elijah, was with us—Jesus, the son of God, in whom God was fully manifest. James, Peter, and I were eyewitnesses.

I was eager to run down the mountain and tell Andrew and the others about it, especially father, for contrary to his fears, I had seen the face of God and lived! The cloud was undoubtedly the presence of the Lord our God, the same that Moses described in his writings. We had heard his voice; witnessed his glory.

"Tell no one yet." Jesus cautioned us. "It is not my Father's time yet!"

And thus, this holy moment that we cherished became a well-kept secret between Peter, James, and me. It was tempting to keep it from Andrew, but then again, Andrew, unwavering in his belief in Jesus, did not need any evidence.

On our way down the mountain, I wondered how we could have seen the face of God and lived. The Holy of Holies in the temple sanctuary was God's dwelling; not even the High Priest could enter without atoning for himself. If we, ordinary fishermen, had seen and heard God, why were our forefathers fearful of the one whose voice had been as gentle as the mother nursing a baby? Why did Jesus ask us not to be afraid? Was not a holy terror of God fundamental to any association with him?

Jesus answered my thoughts. "Perfect love casts out fear, John. Fear has to do with punishment. He who fears has not been made perfect in love."

It took me a lifetime to dig deeper and unearth the treasures of the love that coursed through Jesus' veins. I never forgot it and proclaimed it widely in my later years. Then I was naïve, so were my brothers. We were young and zealous, listening but never hearing, learning from Jesus, yet never understanding.

Under Jesus' tutelage, we gained much ground. He equipped us with the power to win over evil spirits and to heal those who were ravaged by disease. I must admit, it was intoxicating. A spell had been cast upon my heart. Mother, Father, and my days of catching fish and cleaning nets floated into the recesses of the past. I dreamed of the day when the son of God would lead us to a grand victory against Rome.

I could not wait to use my newfound power against our enemies. James and I did not hesitate to call down fire on the Samaritan towns that mocked us in our efforts to spread the word about the Messiah and God's kingdom. Jesus gave James and me the nickname Sons of Thunder, and he was quick to admonish us. "The leaders of the world wield power over others, but you must not be like them!"

We went into the towns and cities in Galilee, bearing witness to the Messiah and his kingdom. At last, we were gathering strength against those who defiled our nation. The Herodians were a thorn in our side just as much as the Romans. Herod Antipas had John the baptizer beheaded in prison. Before his death, John had sent word to Jesus to confirm if he was the Messiah.

Jesus assured John's followers. "Tell John the lame walk, the blind see, and the dead are raised to life."

I hoped these words brought John solace in his last moments. Herod, too, kept a close watch on our movements as reports of Jesus' miracles spread far and wide, too many to recount for not all the scrolls in the world could contain it.

The threat from Rome, the threat at home, no longer deterred me. Armed with a new vision of Jesus, the son of

God, I, along with my brothers, set about to awaken the masses, to reclaim our heritage.

There were many who opened the doors of their hearts and home to us. Jesus enjoyed gathering at the table with folks. Contrary to the norm, he would help our hosts with meal preparations. He enjoyed baking bread. Did he learn that from his mother? Did he miss his family? We never knew; he would point to the crowds saying, "Here are my brothers and sisters and mother."

Yet, all the towns of Galilee, Bethsaida, and Nazareth remained resistant. I was no stranger to the whispers in Bethsaida—"Zebedee's sons are deceived. That wandering preacher has blinded their minds. They will perish under the Roman sword."

At Nazareth, Jesus faced much skepticism from his brothers, who mocked him. "Why don't you do in Judea the miracles you perform openly here in Galilee?" They were aware of the threat that awaited Jesus in Judea, for the temple authorities laid in wait to trap him at an opportune moment.

Jesus held his peace. "It is not my time!"

And then came the time when Jesus instructed us to arrange for a lengthy stay in Judea. As we prepared to travel to Jerusalem for the harvest festival before the winter, not one of us was prepared for the tribulation that awaited us.

14

Jerusalem, 32 AD

A host of pilgrims thronged the temple for the autumn harvest festival, Sukkot, also known as the festival of tents. We camped outside the temple wall for a week, remembering the days that our forefathers roamed the wilderness before they settled in the land which we, their descendants, now occupied. During the festival, our difficulties mounted. The Pharisees engaged Jesus in debate. They were baffled. "How does this man have this much learning when he has never studied under us?"

During one such heated discourse, the Pharisees boasted of their heritage as loyal sons of Abraham—our forefather, through whom our Lord established our nation.

Jesus responded with a bold claim. "Before Abraham was, I am."

"You are demon-possessed!" The Pharisees picked up stones to hurl at Jesus.

The name I am was the name of God, a name we were forbidden to utter, a name by which our Lord identified himself to Moses. It was considered a blasphemy that warranted the death penalty, but Jesus' popularity with the masses made it hard for the authorities to arrest him.

The Pharisees' frustration had mounted. Earlier that day, they had failed to trap Jesus. They had grabbed a woman by her hair as they dragged her across the temple courts. "Teacher, we caught this woman in adultery. What do you say we do?" The teachers knew that the law demanded that she be stoned to death. They were counting on Jesus to acquit her and break the law so they may add to the list of charges they were gathering against him.

Jesus answered, "He who is without sin may cast the first stone." The accusers dropped their stones. They walked away flabbergasted, wallowing in their defeat, for Jesus upheld our laws without rejecting the mercy of God.

Jesus continued teaching and healing under their noses, refusing to turn away the hurting and needy, even on the Sabbath. The authorities were exasperated. "He dishonors Moses; He has no regard for our laws."

Despite these mounting accusations, Jesus healed a blind man on the Sabbath. Unable to contain himself, the man proclaimed his healing with joy. Many who knew him as the blind beggar by the temple gates were astonished and placed their faith in Jesus. The high priest Caiaphas was troubled and sent a delegate of temple guards to arrest Jesus. They turned back and testified. "No one spoke like this man."

I followed them into the temple, concealing myself in the crowd. There was another that made his way in—Judas.

The Sanhedrin sent for the blind man's parents, who confirmed that the man was born blind. The man faced the authorities with boldness. "Jesus is surely a prophet."

Caiaphas and the elders were disturbed and discussed amongst themselves. "Jesus sways the masses and will lead them to destruction; if the wrath of God does not fall upon us first because of this sinner, the fury of Rome shall consume us for the masses may seize him as king and rebel against Rome."

Nicodemus objected. "Can a sinner open the eyes of a man born blind? Does the law permit us to condemn without hearing him out?"

"Can a prophet ever come out of Galilee? Check your scrolls!"

The temple council was divided. Many of the council members favored Jesus yet remained silent for fear of foregoing their seats in the temple assembly. The masses were divided as well. Some mumbled amongst themselves. "Why incur the wrath of the leaders? Not even the Messiah can suppose himself to be God's son!"

Others said, "Should not the authorities who study our scriptures night and day recognize the Messiah and favor his mission for our nation's deliverance?"

I held my tongue. If only we could tell them what we had witnessed on that mountain!

Meanwhile, much to the dismay of the religious leaders, the crowds had found their shepherd. Jesus assured them that a good shepherd would lay down his life for his sheep, unlike the hired hands who ran away when the wolves approached.

Many of the pilgrims who witnessed Jesus' teaching and healing were perplexed. "Is it not the man our authorities seek to kill? Why are they permitting him to speak openly? Have they concluded he is the Messiah?"

The authorities, sensing their grip loosening on the people, seethed in rage and lay in wait for Jesus as a lion for its kill.

That winter, at the feast of Dedication, they tried to capture Jesus. They challenged him to declare if he was the Messiah. He answered them.

"The works I do in my Father's name speak for themselves, but you do not believe me!"

"How dare you, a mere man, claim to be the son of God!" They picked up stones to hurl at him.

The festival of Sukkot to the festival of Pentecost (harvest of first fruits) spanned seven long months. Housed between them was the winter feast of Dedication and the spring Passover celebration. When we left Galilee, we prepared to be in Bethany and Jerusalem for the entire length of this time. However, with the threat to Jesus' life, that winter following the feast of Dedication, we thought it best to retire to the Perean region, south of Galilee and east of the Jordan river, where John the baptizer had many disciples. They sheltered us there until it was time to return to Judea again when our friend Lazarus' servant brought us this message: "The one you love is dying."

15

Bethany, Judea 33 AD

We were hesitant as we made our way back to Judea. "Teacher," we pleaded in unison, "your life is under a grave threat in Judea, yet you are going back?"

Thomas, one of us twelve, threw his hands up in the air. "Let us go with him and die there!"

We had followed Jesus for three years. He had performed many signs, but none that rained fire on our enemies. Despondency had set in amongst some of us. Even Peter, James, and I, who had witnessed the divine affirmation of his authority on Mount Hermon, were wearing out our patience. The threats against us were mounting, yet Jesus did not show urgency in revealing himself as the God-appointed Messiah stating that his time was not at hand. We vacillated between faith and uncertainty, especially when we escaped with our lives on several occasions.

Jesus was firm. "Our friend Lazarus needs us."

Yet, he made no haste to get to Bethany. We waited two days before beginning our travels. Once Jesus had resolved to help his friend, why delay?

As we proceeded towards the home of our friend Lazarus, the sound of wailing greeted us from afar. The townsfolk were beating their breasts. "Oh! To die so young!"

We arrived too late.

Lazarus was loved and respected by the Jews of both Bethany and Jerusalem, which was less than an hour's walk from Bethany. They had gathered to mourn with Mary and Martha.

We learned then that Lazarus had already been in his grave for four days. We arrived in the middle of Shiva—the seven days of grieving post burial. Martha could not contain her disappointment as she rushed to greet us while we were yet a stone's throw away.

"Lord, if you had made haste, my brother would not have died." Her eyes red and puffy, her lips quivering, she pleaded. "I believe you are the Messiah; even now if you ask God, he can raise my brother!"

I marveled at her faith. The dead do not walk, not when they have been under the ground for four days. Peter, James, and I had witnessed Jesus raising a dead girl once, but her body had not yet grown cold. Our friend's body would be cold and stiff, not to mention the stench. Besides, after four days, when the dead have fully crossed over into the afterlife, it is impossible to bring them back. Not even one greater than Moses could do that.

Meanwhile, Mary had come running outside the house to greet us and threw herself at Jesus' feet, shaking and weeping. "Why did you delay?"

Jesus was deeply disturbed in spirit. That was the first time I saw him weep. He lifted her tenderly. "Take me to where you have laid him!"

An enormous crowd followed us to Lazarus' grave. It was a cave with a stone covering its entrance. Some marveled at how much he loved his friend. Others shook their heads and said, "Could he who opened the eyes of the blind man not have kept his friend from dying?"

"Remove the stone," Jesus commanded.

Martha objected. "The odor will be unbearable by now!"

Jesus' eyes softened. "If you believe, you will behold the glory of God, Martha!"

Then Jesus gazed heavenward in praise and thanksgiving to God and called out in a loud voice.

"Lazarus, come forth!"

The hair on the back of my neck stood up. It was the same voice that had commanded the winds and the waves that stormy night. My jaw dropped.

Bound with strips of burial linen, his face covered with the burial cloth, Lazarus emerged from the entrance of his tomb.

Jesus commanded us. "Set him free from the grave clothes!"

But we stood there dumbfounded. The Jews from Jerusalem who had accompanied us to the grave helped untie the linen. They rushed back to bear a report to the high priest and the temple council. Many of them placed their trust in Jesus as the Messiah. News of this miracle spread throughout Judea as a wildfire. Others turned hostile even to Lazarus, whom they once befriended, for he testified freely of Jesus' power and authority despite being instructed otherwise by the leaders.

We received word of an emergency meeting of the Sanhedrin. The council members were distraught and consulted amongst themselves. "If Jesus remains unchecked, the crowds will seize him as a king, and if they march against Rome, our nation and our temple will be decimated!"

Then the high priest, Caiaphas, spoke up. "It is better for a man to die than for a nation to perish."

My blood boiled upon receiving this report. Caiaphas was a wolf. The office of the high priest wielded tremendous social, political, and religious powers, which Caiaphas was careful to secure. He was not from our traditional lineage of priests. His father-in-law, Annas, had been the high priest prior, followed briefly by his brother-in-law, Eleazar, whom Caiaphas replaced after a trip to Rome. I doubted our nation was his primary concern. The procurator of Judea, Pontius Pilate, relied on Caiaphas to uphold peace in the Judean province, which, unlike Galilee, was under the direct jurisdiction of Rome. Any uprisings would register as both Caiaphas and Pilate's failure. The word on the streets of Jerusalem was that Pilate had his sights set on promotion to the courts of Caesar. Surely, he would not leave behind his friend, Caiaphas? It was no wonder then that Caiaphas' anger burned against Jesus, 'a small-town prophet', a boulder in his path, for the crowds were on the verge of making him king.

Caiaphas' fears were justified.

In Galilee, Judea, and even Samaria, word had spread of Jesus bringing Lazarus back from the afterlife. Hundreds of Zealots also joined us. They placed their hope in Jesus to rain fiery plagues from heaven against the prevailing rulers, both those who oppressed us and those who served our oppressors. There was only one thing that continued to puzzle me. What was Jesus waiting for?

As the hostility against us grew, we sought shelter northeast of Jerusalem in the hilly wilderness of the village of Ephraim for a few weeks before we traveled to the temple again for the Passover, which we never neglected to celebrate.

It would be the Passover of a lifetime.

16

Judea, 33 AD
The Jericho Road

The lush oases of Jericho were a welcome change from the wilderness of Ephraim. Caravans of pilgrims jammed the road to Jerusalem, through the town of Jericho. We accompanied them to celebrate yet another Passover. The crowds that followed us were much larger than in previous years. Since Jesus raised Lazarus from the afterlife, many more Jews and Gentiles turned to Jesus, to the dismay of the authorities.

As I walked through Jericho, my stomach fluttered. This was the city whose walls had crumbled in surrender to our forefathers. They fought the battle of Jericho, not with weapons made by hand, but by shouts of praises to our God. Joshua, a leader trained under Moses, led our ancestors to the land God led them to, a land which was bound in chains, but not for long. Our deliverer was here!

As we approached Bethany, where we planned to lodge with Lazarus and his sisters, Jesus instructed us to go ahead of him. "As you enter the next village, you will find a colt with its mother tied there. Untie them and bring them to me.

If anyone asks you, 'Why are you doing this?' say, 'The Lord needs them and will send them back here shortly.'"

We brought the animals to Jesus. He placed his hand on their heads and blessed them. Then he lifted his eyes towards Jerusalem and said, "Do not be afraid, daughter of Zion; see, your king is coming, seated on a donkey's colt."

My ears perked up. God's kingdom was at hand. Soon, we would march against the rulers in the temple, who defiled it by bowing before Rome, cleansing it once and for all.

Bethany

The enemy at home proved more tiresome than Rome. We arrived in Bethany before Sabbath set in, six days ahead of the Passover feast. The villagers flocked to greet us when they learned Jesus lodged at Lazarus' home. Nicodemus had warned us that though many waited with fervor for Jesus to arrive at the festival, there were many more who were instructed by the chief priest and the Pharisees to report Jesus' whereabouts so they might arrest him ahead of the festival to avoid riots. They wanted to kill Lazarus also, for it was because of his witness that Jesus' following in Jerusalem grew. Our leaders turned a blind eye to Jesus' wondrous deeds while their ears burned with his praises.

Mary and Martha set a feast to honor Jesus. As we reclined at the table, Mary poured a pint of pure nard at Jesus' feet.

Judas shook his head. "Why waste all of this expensive perfume? We could have sold it and used the money to help the poor!"

Andrew was reclining next to me; he held me back from punching Judas.

"How dare he!" I whispered to Andrew, "we must relieve him of the charge of the money bag; He uses it to lather himself with expensive scents. He does not care for the poor."

There was one thing I wish I had confided in Andrew then—Judas' peculiar movements. He had sneaked out of the house the previous night after dinner and not returned till the wee hours of the morning. I lay awake, flustered. I wondered if he was conducting a secret meeting with the Zealots. If they picked up their swords ahead of Jesus' time to march against the rulers, their blood would flow like a river. I shuddered. If only they would wait. Jesus was sure to deliver.

Jesus turned to Judas. "Leave her alone. She has anointed my body for burial." His words made my heart sink. What did he mean? Moses did not die (although some say he did and God buried his body), and a chariot of fire took the prophet Elijah up to heaven; surely, the Messiah greater than them could not die. Perhaps this was yet another one of his parables, which he would explain to us in private. I was hopeful the authorities could not lay hands on Jesus. However, this did not keep me from pondering what they might do to us, his disciples.

Jerusalem

The second day after the Sabbath, we made our way to Jerusalem. As we ascended the Mount of Olives, the air was crisp. My heart burst in song as I saw Jesus seated on the donkey, with its colt beside it. The terrain was rough and unsuitable for a young colt to bear the burden of a traveler. We took off our cloaks and placed them on the donkey as a seat for Jesus. His face was glowing, his eyes kind yet as lightning. The crowds rushed to greet him as their king, throwing their cloaks before him and laying his path with palm branches which they also waved shouting, "Hosanna- blessed is he who comes in the name of the Lord!"

As we descended into the valley of Kidron and drew near the temple gates, the crowds roared and cheered. "Blessed is the coming kingdom of our messiah, hosanna in the highest heaven!"

Jerusalem was stirred with the praises of Jesus. The Pharisees were alarmed. "Look! The whole world has been deceived and runs after him!"

They rushed out to rebuke us as we approached the city. "Ask the mob to be quiet!"

Jesus addressed them with boldness. "If you silence the people, the stones will cry out!"

His heart heavy, his eyes moist, Jesus cried out in a loud voice, "Oh, Jerusalem! How I longed to gather you under my wings as a hen gathers her chicks! If you had only known on this day what would bring you peace—but now it is hidden from your eyes until you accept the favor of your God through his chosen one!"

I took his words to mean a declaration of war against the temple leaders for defiling the house of God, for not favoring the Messiah in his mission. If only they would relinquish their unbelief and support our mission of re-establishing a free nation beholden to none but our God.

When we arrived at the city walls, Jesus rode the colt into Jerusalem. The temple was buzzing as usual with worshippers who arrived early to purchase the Passover lamb ahead of the sacrifice and feast. Once again, Jesus drove out those who were making profits from swindling pilgrims. He was indignant. "My house will be a house of prayer, but you have made it a den of robbers."

Some animals escaped, taking advantage of the commotion that followed. The bleating of goats and lambs filled the temple courts as they ran helter-skelter while their sellers tried to chase them down. The merchants swore revenge and joined the leaders who opposed Jesus.

The chief priests, the teachers of the law, and the leaders of the people were boiling over, yet unable to lay a hand on Jesus, for the masses would not leave him alone. There were many Greeks among them from non-Jewish provinces. Andrew brought them to Jesus.

Deeply moved by the faith of the Gentiles, Jesus stood up to pray. "For this hour, I came into the world. The time has come for you to honor me, my Father. Unless a kernel of wheat falls to the ground, it remains only a seed. It cannot bear many seeds unless it dies. Who seeks to save his life will lose it, and one who loses his life for my sake will find it. Father, glorify your name!"

There was thunder from heaven. I discerned the voice of God in it. "I have glorified it and will do it again!"

My eyes grew wide. I stifled a scream. It was a battle cry.

17

Jerusalem, 33 AD

The Afternoon of the Passover Feast

"I have eagerly desired to eat this Passover with you before I suffer." Jesus appeared grim.

In times past, he had celebrated with us at large gatherings. All our families were in Judea for the celebrations, but Jesus requested a private meal with us. Jesus sent Peter and me into the holy city with the instructions: "As you enter the city, a man carrying a jar of water will meet you. Follow him to the house that he enters, and say to the owner of the house, 'The Teacher asks: Where is the guest room, where I may eat the Passover with my disciples?' He will show you a large room upstairs, all furnished. Make preparations there."

Peter and I set about to obey his instructions. Jesus' earlier statement had me downcast—Why did he request a private meal? What does he mean by 'before I suffer'?

I confided in Peter. He shook his head and grinned.

"You overthink! Has the teacher not suffered enough at the hands of the leaders? Did you not hear him say his time was near? Perhaps we will march to Jerusalem soon and suffer opposition there, but surely as God's favored one, the teacher will lead us in victory! Maybe, he requests a private meal to instruct us for battle. You have waited for this moment!"

Indeed, I had. The Messiah's appointed time had come. He had said so! None of us knew the exact moment. However, I could not shake off the feelings of dread that loomed over me. Jitters, perhaps.

The Evening of the Passover Feast

That evening, as we reclined at the table in the upper room prepared by the owners of the house, John Mark and his mother, my heart was full as I leaned on Jesus' bosom. He occupied the host's seat to my left. My eyes scanned the perimeter of the oval table around which all my brothers reclined; across from me was Peter, then James, Thomas, Nathaniel, also called Bartholomew, Philip, and Matthew. Andrew was sitting at the tip of the table in the farthest left corner. On my side, to my extreme left, was Simon, followed by the other Judas, the other James, and Judas the Zealot to Jesus' immediate left, a seat reserved for the guest of honor. I felt a surge of anger. Who invited him to occupy the seat?

Judas appeared grim and distant; My distrust of him had grown. However, I set aside my anger. It was a time of joyous fellowship with Jesus and my brothers. I would not let Judas ruin it. We, the disciples, were family. Soon, we would march alongside each other to overthrow our oppressors. We were close to our mission, a moment to celebrate, not brood.

I leaned on Jesus. His heart was beating in a steady rhythm. Mine was racing. Could Jesus hear it? As we began our meal, I marveled at how graciously Jesus served us. He nodded as he passed me by while serving the lamb. "You will not have to suffer this again, John!" His words baffled me. Was he going to abolish the lamb sacrifice when he cleansed the temple? Not even he could revoke the mandate of our God. I pictured my father shaking his head when I refused to partake of the Passover sacrifice. I smiled. What my father thought no longer mattered.

Light-hearted chatter and hearty laughter dominated the dinner conversation. But as storms arise on the Sea of Galilee without warning, a squabble arose amongst us. We sensed that the time was upon us to accompany Jesus on his mission to restore our nation's glory. We expected he would assign us different roles in this new kingdom; James and I requested to be at Jesus' right and left hand. The rest of the disciples were indignant. They implored Jesus.

"We have left everything to follow you; what's in it for us?"

Jesus admonished us. "Do not be like the rulers who wield power over the people!" Instead, the greatest among you should be like the one who serves. For who is greater, the one who is at the table, or the one who serves? Is it not the one who is at the table? Look! I am among you as one who serves; do as I do!"

Jesus assured us. His voice was kind, yet somber. "You are those who have stood by me in my trials. And I confer on you a kingdom, as my Father conferred one on me, so that you may eat and drink at my table in my kingdom and sit on thrones, judging the twelve tribes of Israel."

Jubilant exclamations filled the room: "He will grant us thrones according to the descendants of the twelve tribes that comprised the first seeds of our nation from the children of our forefather Jacob. We will be judges and rulers!"

Jesus shook his head and sighed. He removed his outer cloak, tied a towel around his waist, walked up to Peter, and washed his feet, an act fit only for a servant.

Peter gasped and cried in a loud voice. "You must not wash my feet!"

The commotion in the room died down. All eyes were on Jesus.

"Do you understand what I have done for you? If I, your teacher, have washed your feet, you must do this for one another."

None looked him in the eye nor spoke a word as, one by one, he washed all our feet.

As Jesus cleansed the dirt off my feet, I stared into Jesus' eyes. They were my mother's eyes—the same tender affection. Mother would wipe my feet when I returned home after a hard day on the sea. I shifted my gaze to his hands that were busy wiping my feet with his towel. I wondered if this Jesus was the same one who transformed into the divine son of God on that high mountain that day?

From that moment, none of us ever asked "who will be great in your kingdom?" For the greatest one among us had lowered himself to a servant's estate.

We resumed our meal in silence until Jesus' kind affirmation revived our spirit. "You are to serve one another, but I have not treated you as servants. A servant does not know his master's business. I have revealed to you all that my Father has revealed to me, so you are not servants but my friends!" This gladdened our hearts. However, then Jesus said something that alarmed us. "One of you will betray me!" Determined not to start yet another altercation, we muttered and whispered amongst ourselves. "Who can it be?"

Peter motioned to me to ask Jesus since I was leaning on Jesus as we reclined. Jesus answered me, speaking softly so only Peter and I could hear. "It is the one who dips his hand in the bowl of bread with me."

It was Judas.

Before I could respond, Jesus took the bread, broke it, and distributed it amongst us, saying, "Take and eat as a remembrance of my body, which is broken for you!" No one asked him "what do you mean?" We were busy with dinner. Besides, Jesus often spoke in parables and expounded upon them, eventually.

After our dinner he passed a cup of wine, saying, "This is the cup of a new covenant sealed by my blood which is poured out for you!" His voice was somber.

We shook our heads, struggling to make sense of Jesus' words.

Then Jesus turned to Judas and said, "Go, do what you must!"

I understood this to mean that Jesus was permitting him to go join the Zealots since the speed at which Jesus was progressing on our mission disgruntled Judas. The others understood Judas was off to make further preparations for the rest of the festival since he had charge of the money bag.

After Judas left, Jesus declared yet again that the time had come for him to honor his Father's desire to establish his kingdom. His words ought to have elated me, but the sense of foreboding beneath them weighed me down.

My unrest grew as Jesus continued to caution us. "A time is coming when you all will be cast out of the synagogues; those who seek to spill your blood will consider it an offering to God and compel you to sell your cloaks to buy swords."

"Why would we need swords, if we have you?" I chimed in.

"I am with you only for a little while, John!"

"We will follow you, wherever it is you are going!" Peter burst out.

"Where I am going, you cannot come. All of you will be scattered on account of me, especially you, Peter. Jesus' tone was grim. You will deny me three times before the rooster crows."

Peter was distressed upon hearing this and shook his head in disbelief.

Thomas asked, "Where are you going? Show us the way!"

"I am going to my Father, Thomas, and I am the way to him."

"Then show us the Father," Philip pleaded.

"I have been with you so long, Philip, and yet you do not know me? He who has seen me has seen the Father!"

"Lord, you cannot leave us now!" I beseeched Jesus.

"My children, it is only for a little while that I will be away from you; I go to prepare a place for you so you can be with me in my Father's house forever. Besides, if I do not go, the helper cannot come. I will not leave you as orphans; I will send the helper. He will lead you in truth and comfort; take heart. I leave my peace with you, and since I have overcome the world, you will too!"

His manner was gentle, yet resolute. It cheered me up momentarily, but my mind was unsettled with the ebb and flow of thoughts: Who was the helper? Was he like Moses' helper Aaron? Why was Jesus going to get him? One moment the teacher speaks of leading us in battle, establishing the kingdom and then he talks of leaving us? What did he mean by 'I will be away only a little while.'?

Then he admonished us like a mother before she leaves on a long journey without her children. "I leave this new command with you, love one another as I have loved you; by this, you will show yourselves to be my true disciples!"

Then he prayed for our protection, blessings, unity, and that all may believe in our message of his kingdom, and that most of all we would know his love—of which I needed no persuading. Of all the times I doubted Jesus, I never once doubted his love for us. However, I wondered why he did not ask God to unleash the angel armies for our aid. I sensed we were going to need them soon.

18

Gethsemane, Mount of Olives near Jerusalem, 33 AD
The Night of the Passover Feast

I threw a blanket over my outer cloak and pulled it up to my face, covering my nose and mouth. The spring air had a distinct chill. Our host, John Mark, had provided us with extra blankets as we departed his home, where we had celebrated our Passover feast. We had closed with a hymn of praise which lightened our hearts, otherwise laden with a sense of impending sorrow because of Jesus' words of caution. The crisp air and the walk to the mount of olives restored our mood. We were glad when Jesus stopped at the grove where he often retired to pray alone and bid us halt there. Andrew and the others lit a fire and laid their blankets in a clearing amidst the trees.

Jesus motioned to Peter, James, and me to follow him, as he walked a stone's throw away from the others. His voice cracked. "Keep watch with me; my soul is overwhelmed with sorrow."

But alas, the dinner had worked its way from our bellies to our eyelids. We could barely keep them open. The sound of crickets and the warmth of the fire lulled us to slumber. We took turns to stay awake with Jesus. Peter snored while James struggled to keep his head from wobbling. I sat upright, clutching my blanket, having volunteered for the first watch. I heard him praying with loud cries and tears. "Father, take this cup away from me! Yet, not my will but yours be done."

The garden was dark save for the light of the moon, peeking through the cloud cover, falling on Jesus' face where he knelt. I saw his veins bulging. Large drops of dark liquid fell from his brows to the ground. His sweat had turned to blood. I saw a being by his side comforting him. Was it an angel? I got up to draw near him but staggered and fell. My body had stiffened. The wholesome meal and the excitement of the day had depleted my strength. Jesus was in anguish, yet I could not move. Despite my best efforts to keep him company, I drifted off to sleep.

"John, Peter, James, wake up! Can you not keep watch with me!" Jesus tapped my shoulder. Then he walked a little further, dropped to his knees, covered his face, and prayed once more. I could hear his loud cries. "If this cup cannot be taken from me, then I must drink from it, Father!"

I perceived his agony, though I failed to understand it. It was as though I wrestled with a nightmare. He tapped me on the shoulder again. I did not budge. Jesus spoke with compassion, "The spirit is willing, but the flesh is weak." He went back to pray. But, by this time, I had shaken off my sleep. I could not perceive what had gotten a hold of him, for I had never witnessed him in this kind of anguish—ever.

Jesus approached me, his face shining. He was at peace. There was a glint in his eyes. It was not from the light of the moon. "Let us wake the others. Here comes my betrayer to have me arrested!"

My heart was in my mouth. Out of the shadows of the olive trees emerged several figures with torches, lanterns, clubs, and swords. Their leader was Judas.

By this time, the twelve of us were wide awake and crowded around Jesus. What followed was a whirlwind. The chief priest and the elders had commissioned the Roman soldiers and temple guards to arrest Jesus in the stealth of the night. I recognized Malchus, servant of the high priest Caiaphas.

Jesus asked, "who do you seek?"

They replied, "Jesus of Nazareth."

Jesus said, "I am he; let the others go" The soldiers drew back, and the temple guards fell on the ground as if knocked over by an unseen force.

They got back on their feet to arrest Jesus but could not see where he stood because a dark cloud had covered the moon. Then Judas walked to Jesus and greeted him with a kiss. This was a signal to the men who arrested Jesus. I clenched my fist. How could Judas betray us? How many coins did he add to his moneybag? I wished to use a sword if only to chop off Judas' neck. Peter, however, was swift to draw his sword and strike Malchus, chopping off his ear. Jesus placed his hands on Malchus and healed his ear in an instant. Malchus fell to the ground. His eyes met Jesus. Jesus lifted him and turned to Peter. "Put your sword away, Peter! All who draw the sword will die by it. Shall I not drink from the cup ordained by my Father? Do you think I cannot call on my Father, and he will at once put at my disposal more than twelve legions of angels?"

Was this moment of glory he had spoken of earlier? Would he call on angels and rain fire from heaven? He turned to the temple guards and said, "Am I leading a rebellion that you have come out with swords and clubs to capture me? Every day I sat in the temple courts teaching, and you did not arrest me. But this has all taken place to fulfill the writings of the prophets. This is your hour when darkness reigns!"

And darkness was unleashed, not only on Jesus but also on us. As Jesus had predicted earlier that evening, each one of us fled in different directions. James and Andrew took off to Bethany to bear the news to Jesus' mother and brothers, who lodged at Lazarus' home for the Passover. I followed Jesus along with the band of those who apprehended him. He had allowed himself to be bound willingly. I needed to determine what Jesus had planned. Peter followed me from afar.

It was the beginning of an endless night.

19

Jerusalem, 33 AD

The sudden turn of events left me reeling. I hoped we would return to Galilee after the Passover, unscathed, for the authorities would not dream of disturbing the peace in the city when it was overflowing with pilgrims and Roman soldiers. The governor, Pontius Pilate, was also visiting Jerusalem. Why arrest Jesus now?

The excitement of the past few days had barely died down. The masses had hailed Jesus as our king and were ready for him to lead us in deliverance. Jesus himself had declared that his kingdom was imminent. Why, then, did Jesus not resist his arrest? Where were the armies of angels? Where was the fiery rain? Was Jesus going to establish his kingdom by a miracle, even after his arrest?

I kept a close distance from Jesus even as they led him away. The moon hid behind a dense cloud. I pulled my blanket over my face and slipped in with the mob that led Jesus to the home of Caiaphas' father-in-law, Annas, who was also a reputed ruler of the people.

Peter had followed me into the courtyard, where he concealed himself among the servants who warmed themselves by the fire. I drew closer to Jesus. The council members of the Sanhedrin surrounded him in the outer room, facing the courtyard. Some of them muttered curses while some wrung their hands. Others shook their heads and pointed to Jesus, shaking their fists. I could not see Jesus, but the distinct sound of his chains alerted me to his whereabouts. Annas paced the room. A tiny lamp in the corner of the room cast his giant shadow on the wall. He turned to Jesus; his voice was as ice. "What have you been teaching the people?"

"Why do you question me? I have taught in the open. Ask those who have heard me speak."

One of the council members who stood next to Jesus slapped him. "Is this how you speak to the ruler of your people?"

Jesus replied, "Can you deny what I said? If not, why do you strike me for speaking the truth?"

Then Nicodemus came forward. "The law does not permit us to prosecute a man without the testimony of at least two or three witnesses."

Annas commanded the guards. "Go, bring those who have agreed to bear witness!"

The witnesses appeared with their rehearsed testimonies; some were merchants whose tables Jesus had overturned at the temple. Others received bribes. "This man said he will destroy the temple of God and rebuild it in three days!"

The Sanhedrin was not in agreement. Among those who objected to the witnesses were Nicodemus and Joseph from the town of Arimathea. Unable to reach a verdict, Annas handed the matter to Caiaphas.

"Are you not going to answer?" Caiaphas bellowed. "What is this testimony that these men are bringing against you?" Exasperated by Jesus' silence, Caiaphas continued, "I charge you under oath by the living God. Tell us if you are the Messiah, the Son of God."

"You have said so," Jesus replied. "But I say to all of you. From now on, you will see the Son of Man sitting at the right hand of the Mighty One and coming on the clouds of heaven."

Then Caiaphas tore his clothes and said, "He has spoken blasphemy! Why do we need any more witnesses? Your own ears bear testimony. What do you think?"

The others of the Sanhedrin drowned the voices of Nicodemus and Joseph. "This man is worthy of death."

Then the guards blindfolded him, spit in his face, pulled his beard, and struck him with their fists. Others slapped him and said, "Prophesy to us, Messiah. Who hit you?"

My blood ran cold. Is this the one who commanded the winds and the waves that night in the storm? Panic set in. What will become of him? What will become of us? Have the leaders been right all along? Is he the Messiah? Did we hallucinate on the mountain that day when Jesus transformed before our eyes?

A commotion in the courtyard interrupted my musings. Peter was shaking his fist at the servants and hurling insults at them. He took off shouting, "I do not know the man!" Not perceiving what the altercation was about, I contemplated running after Peter, but I could not budge. Despite my disappointment with Jesus, I found myself tied to him with cords of brotherhood. I hoped Peter would run back to the others and update them on the events of the evening. I resolved to be by Jesus' side.

Just then, I heard the rooster crow for the second time. It was the third hour, six hours past midnight, on the day before the sabbath. I heard Caiaphas announce, "We shall take him to Pilate."

Those scheming devils!

The authorities had waited three years to kill Jesus. Unable to lay a hand on him in the open, their frustration had mounted. They employed the traitor from amidst us to deliver Jesus to them in the quiet of the night. They had charged Jesus with blasphemy, a crime punishable by death. However, resistance from the masses could hinder their plans. Besides, in times past, disturbances in the temple courts have led to Roman soldiers rushing in with their swords. The authorities were careful to avoid bloodshed during the festival. Therefore, they devised a plan to have Jesus condemned by Rome and spare them the responsibility of his blood.

The sabbath would set in that evening. They could not touch Jesus then. Then it dawned on me.

They would execute Jesus before sundown.

20

Jerusalem, 33 AD
The Temple

The Sanhedrin charged Jesus with treason and blasphemy, and he showed no signs to deliver himself by signs or miracles. Was he under the spell of delusion? If only I had trained in the sword. I could hear Peter and James in my head. 'An eye for an eye, John!' If only I had listened. If only I could chop off a few heads, even if it meant losing mine! We had followed him to a fool's paradise, and yet, I continued to follow him to the Antonia citadel, to the palace where Pilate had taken residence for the week of the festival to oversee peace in the city.

I raced ahead of the crowd to get to the fortress using a shortcut through the temple, connected to the Antonia fortress by bridges, stairways, and underground passages.

To my surprise, I ran into Mary, Jesus' mother, Mary of Magdala, and my mother. The others had alerted them of our troubles, and they supposed the Sanhedrin would try Jesus at the temple. Jesus' mother's eyes searched mine. "Where is he?"

"They are taking him to Pilate!" I answered, holding Mary's hand lest she should collapse.

But Mary was as stone, her eyes as bronze. Her voice was steady. "This is the hour when a sword shall pierce my soul, as the prophet at the temple foretold shortly after his birth."

I wanted to sink into my mother's arms and weep, but there was no time for that.

Antonia Fortress

The chief priests and elders gathered outside the palace inside the fortress, shaking their fingers vehemently at Jesus and hurling insults at him. They refrained from entering the palace of the Gentiles, for the Sabbath was about to set in, and this would deem them unclean. I marveled how their conscience was seared towards the law yet hardened towards the murder of an innocent man.

Pilate came out to the courtyard. I suspect it was not as much to please our leaders, but he too had heard of Jesus' miracles and wanted to check him out for himself. He had likely been awakened from his slumber and was disgruntled. He sized Jesus from head to toe. A flicker of mockery appeared in his smile. "Try him by your laws. Why bring a Jew to me?"

The elders stood firm in their fierce allegations. "He had committed treason against Rome! He instigates the masses and refuses to pay taxes to Caesar; He says he is a king and the son of God! You must prosecute him to the fullest extent of the Roman law."

Pilate was wide awake by then. He turned to Jesus. "Are you a king?"

Jesus replied, "my kingdom belongs to another world. If I were a king in this world, my followers would have resisted my arrest, but as it stands, they cause no trouble for you!"

Pilate tilted his head and peered at Jesus. "You are a king, then!"

Jesus replied, "It is you who say so. I was born into this world to testify and uphold the truth."

At this statement, Pilate threw his head back and laughed. "What is truth? A mere chasing after the wind. Do you hear the charges against you? You know I have the authority to release you or set you free? Why do you not speak in your defense?

"You have no authority except the one granted to you by my Father above." Pilate paused and thought for a moment, deeming Jesus' words to be those of a man who had suffered both from lack of sleep and hunger. Turning to the crowds, he declared, "this man may be delirious, at best, but I do not find any evidence for your charges!"

The priests and elders, fearing losing ground once again, shook their fists and shouted louder. "This man is no friend of the empire. His followers have been plotting a rebellion against the imperial authorities. He had misled the masses from Galilee to Judea. If you befriend him, then you are no friend of Caesars."

Pilate turned to Jesus. "Are these charges true?"

Jesus remained silent. Pilate sat down; his brows raised, his lips pursed. Then his face lit up. "He is from Galilee, you say? Then, this case is not under my jurisdiction. Let Herod try him."

Pilate was careful not to draw the attention of Rome to himself. His past brush with the emperor had been unfavorable, and he could not afford controversies to ruin his political ambitions. He could neither befriend nor find fault with Jesus. It was most beneficial for Pilate that Jesus was a Galilean and Herod, ruler of Galilee, was in Judea for the Passover.

Herod's Palace

Herod resented Pilate for Pilate occupied a position that had once belonged to Herod's father, ruler of Judea. Herod was puffed up that Pilate should seek his favor. Besides, he had been waiting to see the much-talked-about 'Prophet from Galilee.'

Herod demanded Jesus perform signs and wonders, but Jesus did not respond. Herod scorned him. "Are you king of the Jews?"

Jesus did not utter a word. Then, Herod resorted to ridiculing him. His men paraded Jesus in purple robes and mocked him. Jesus did not retaliate. That rascal, Herod, had John the baptizer executed. I doubted he would spare Jesus. However, to my surprise, Herod decided the evidence against Jesus was insufficient, and the chief priests and elders led him to Pilate once again.

Antonia Fortress

Pilate was pacing across the courtyard outside his palace. He summoned the leaders of our people and said, "Herod finds no credible charge against this man, Jesus, and neither do I. My wife has also been tormented in a dream and sent me a warning 'have nothing to do with that righteous man.' Jesus has done nothing to deserve the death penalty. Suffice it to have him flogged."

Pilate hoped that flogging Jesus would please our rulers and prevent them from reporting Pilate to Rome as one who made light of the grave crime of treason for which they continued to accuse Jesus. Pilate despised our leaders.

He perceived they wanted Jesus dead for their gain, and he resolved not to give in to them.

The soldiers scourged Jesus with ropes that had metal balls and spikes, ripping his flesh to shreds and exposing his bones, but it did not satisfy the blood lust of those who hated him. They shouted even louder, challenging Pilate. "If you befriend him, you are no friend of Caesar!"

Pilate threw his hands up in the air and turned to the crowds. "Do you want me to release your king to you?" It was Rome's custom to release a prisoner to us once every year at the festival.

But the masses rejected Jesus. Some exchanged loyalty for a handsome sum of money, while others lost hope he was the Messiah because he did not fight back or call down fire. Many were swayed by the accusations against Jesus, while the Zealots wanted their leader, Barabbas, back. Barabbas was an insurrectionist and a murderer. The people shouted. "Give us Barabbas instead!"

Pilate shouted. "What do you want me to do with Jesus?"

"Crucify him!"

The more Pilate pleaded, the louder they roared. "Away with him!"

I sank to the ground. With the crowd turning against us, Jesus' execution was imminent. I could not believe what I had just witnessed. The Roman governor had shown more kindness than my people.

Exasperated at their determination to murder an innocent man, and fearing another revolt, Pilate ordered a basin of water, washed his hands, and announced, "I am not guilty of this man's blood; you are responsible." Pilate summoned a garrison of soldiers. "Prepare him for crucifixion!"

The soldiers led Jesus into the palace. They threw a purple robe on him, set a crown made of thorns on his forehead, and mocked him. "Hail, king of the Jews!" They struck him on the head over and over with a staff and spit on his face.

"Stop it! This man has suffered enough!" The commander of the garrison thundered. It was Flavius Marcus. He was the same centurion whose servant Jesus had healed. He had worked his way up the ranks and was commander over the soldiers in Jerusalem.

His eyes met mine. Then he looked down. He was no different from me.

We were both slaves.

21

Jerusalem, 33 AD

Mount Calvary, Golgotha

I followed Jesus to the mound of Calvary outside the city walls, squeezing through the narrow streets of Jerusalem, further cramped with guards lined on both sides. The crowds squeezed through to glimpse the procession of those sentenced to crucifixion—Jesus, along with two thieves, each carrying their heavy wooden beams on which they would suffer and die.

The soldiers prodded Jesus as cattle. Jesus, who made the lame walk, staggered under the weight of the beams. He had lost a lot of blood already. I made haste to aid him, but the guards had already commanded one known as Simon of Cyrene to carry Jesus' cross.

It was the third hour. The smoke from the morning sacrifice of the unblemished lamb rose from the temple in the distance. Jesus' scream pierced my heart as the soldiers drove the nails through his wrists and feet.

Pilate had ordered a board placed over Jesus' head with this charge written in Aramaic, Greek, and Latin—"This is

Jesus, King of the Jews." Our leaders demanded changing it to "This man claimed to be King of the Jews."

But Pilate did not concede. "I have written what I have written."

In a twist of fate, Pilate had been the only person who showed a hint of softness towards Jesus. Even those who had witnessed Jesus raise Lazarus from the dead demanded that Jesus be put to death. Jesus' words to the soldiers who arrested him in Gethsemane rang true: "This is the hour that darkness rules!"

The soldiers who jeered at him stripped him of his garments and cast lots for it. Killing, shaming, and eroding the dignity of those they assaulted were routine for these men, except Flavius Marcus. His face was flushed and dripping sweat. He offered Jesus some wine mixed with vinegar to dull the pain, but Jesus refused, as though he embraced the suffering in its entirety. Jesus looked down at Flavius and his men and cried in a loud voice. "Father forgive them, for they do not know what they are doing!" Flavius hung his head, tears streaming down his face.

Meanwhile, the teachers of our laws smirked as they hurled insults upon Jesus. "He said he will tear down the temple; he cannot even come down from the cross! Even now, if he saves himself, we will believe he is the Messiah!"

Liars! Murderers!

I had been wavering between hope and doubt regarding Jesus being the Messiah, but this one thing I never doubted — Jesus was no criminal. Yet, he suffered as one. The two thieves were crucified with him, one on each side.

A flurry of thoughts haunted me: Jesus is no Moses. If not him, then who? He commands winds and waves; demons tremble at the sound of his voice; he raises the dead. Why does he not call upon the angel armies? He may not be the Messiah, but he is no ordinary man! Why then does he subject himself to the will of the ordinary?

Surely, our God has forsaken his people. Father was right. Chasing after freedom is futile.

Jesus' mother, Mary, had been clinging to me this whole time, lifeless, her lips parched, and eyes swollen. The other Mary from Magdala and my mother were there with us. Poor Mother! She had held out hope for a Messiah, one like Moses long before I was born. I fought back my tears. It was then that Jesus finally spoke and gave me charge of his mother.

I watched him suffer on that wooden pole, his body caving under the fluid that was filling in his chest. That was when Abel came to mind. With each Passover spent with Jesus, Abel had become a distant memory until that day—when I stood witness to the innocent one pierced on a pole. I had betrayed Abel. This time, however, I felt betrayed.

I burst into tears. How could I doubt Jesus' love for me? I pleaded with heaven. "I cannot bear to see him suffer!"

And heaven showed mercy. As the sun was about to take its noon-time position in the sky, thick, black clouds rolled in, shielding it and plunging us into blinding darkness. I could not even see Mary, who was right beside me. Thankfully, I could no longer see Jesus suffer, either.

The unexpected darkness caused the crowds to panic. The soldiers, fearing a stampede, commanded that none move from their place until the darkness passed. Pain and stiffness had set in my back. No food or drink had passed my lips, nor had my eyes known any sleep since the previous evening. My knees gave way as I hit the ground. I do not know how long I lay there. When I came around, it was still dark. I could hear Jesus' breath get heavier. When the darkness lifted, the smoke was rising from the afternoon temple offering of the unblemished lamb. It was three hours past noon.

Then Jesus cried in a loud voice. "My Father, my Father, why have you forsaken me?"

My heart broke. At last, I understood. Perhaps it was God who removed his favor from his chosen Messiah. Is that why Jesus suffered so, emptied of his divine powers, unable to help himself and us? Had the transgressions of our rulers caused God to turn away? Did this mean that our nation would be in bondage forever?

Darkness, deeper than the one that had just lifted from the earth, penetrated my being.

Then I heard Jesus say, "I thirst!" Flavius rushed to instruct his men to soak a sponge with wine vinegar and hold it up to Jesus' lips on the stalk of a hyssop plant.

Overcome by a sudden surge of energy, Jesus cried in a loud voice, "It is finished! Father, into your hands, I commit my spirit!"

With that, he bowed his head and gave up his spirit.

The earth shook; the veil in the holy of holies split in two. I was seized with terror. Had the wrath of God befallen us?

Flavius voiced my thoughts. "The heavens deny us their favor. Surely we have killed a righteous man!"

The people also beat their breasts, but it was too late.

The special Passover sabbath was about to set in. Our leaders requested Jesus' body be brought down from the cross before the Sabbath. The soldiers ventured to hasten his death by breaking his legs, as was their norm; However, when they realized Jesus was already dead, they refrained from breaking his bones. One of the soldiers pierced his side with a spear, to be sure, and a sudden rush of water and blood gushed out.

Mary, his mother, gave out a cry of anguish and sank into my arms.

The Cave in the Garden Near Golgotha

Joseph of Arimathea requested permission from Pilate to take charge of Jesus' body, which Pilate granted. Nicodemus assisted Joseph in preparing the body for burial. They anointed his body with myrrh and aloe, which Nicodemus had generously supplied. Mary, Jesus' mother, and the women who accompanied us helped wipe the blood off of his body. Mary, his mother, wiped the blood from his brow, where the crown of thorns had pierced it, with her shawl. She folded it and held it to her chest.

Joseph and Nicodemus wrapped Jesus' body in clean linen strips as per custom and made their way to a nearby garden where Joseph had a tomb recently built for himself in a rocky cave. I followed them there with the women who were with me. Joseph and Nicodemus laid Jesus to rest.

Mary of Magdala sat by the entrance to the tomb and wept till the sun went down. The Sabbath had begun; she and the other women went to prepare spices for the burial rituals. I took off in the crowd that followed the temple council to the Antonia fortress once again. I was overcome with grief but determined to stay ahead of their devices.

Antonia Fortress

Our leaders had heard rumors that Jesus had said that the temple he would rebuild in three days was his body. Now, Jesus himself had spoken these words to us, but after the loss of his divine power upon that cross, I did not believe so—I doubted any of the other disciples did either. But to the authorities, Jesus remained a threat even in his grave.

They appealed to Pilate. "You must secure his tomb for his disciples may steal his body and hide it and spread rumors he is alive after the third day. This deception will be far more dangerous!"

Pilate ordered Flavius Marcus to have his men secure the tomb till the third day. I followed them to the cave where Jesus lay. It took sixteen soldiers to roll a large round slab of stone to seal the entrance to the tomb. One centurion under Flavius, Petronius, took charge of the operation. He and one of his men stood by either side of the stone, keeping watch through the night.

Even in death, they could not let Jesus rest. What then would become of us?

22

The Sabbath, Passover, 33 AD

I left all the women in the care of my mother in Jerusalem. I rushed back to Bethany, to the home of Lazarus and his sisters. I hoped to find my brothers there.

It was a little past midnight. Peter rushed to greet me. He broke down. "I have betrayed him!" His tears soaked my cloak as I embraced him. Then he recounted to me how he had disowned Jesus three times in the courtyard of the high priest, fearing they might arrest him too. The servant girl had been quick to point him out to others as one of Jesus' disciples, and he had sworn before them he did not know Jesus. That explained the altercation I had witnessed.

"It was not you, Peter. It was that devil Judas! If only I could lay my hands on him."

"Too late!" Andrew had joined us. "That coward sold us for thirty pieces of silver and now lies dead; he hanged himself!"

I sat down. My feet hurt. Finding myself safe with my brothers, I could finally give in to my grief. My brothers gathered around me as I recounted the events of the past twenty-four hours. Upon hearing the atrocities inflicted upon

Jesus, James picked up his sword. "Caiaphas and the elders must pay with blood!"

Andrew held him back. "Did you not hear what John said? The masses are no longer with us! Besides, didn't Jesus say he could call ten thousand angels? But he didn't. God has turned away from us; perhaps this nation does not deserve deliverance, for its leaders continue to slumber in sin and transgression against the Lord by submitting themselves to the will of its rulers. Their reward is servitude to foreigners!"

That was the first time I heard Andrew speak against hope. The roller coaster of the past three years had caught up with us all: the thrill of following one like Moses, the miracles, signs and wonders, the affection of the masses and ridicule from our townsfolk, fleeing for our lives often, confrontation with the leaders and elders and ultimately a failed mission and a savior who was reluctant to save himself, and a God who had forsaken his people. Indeed, hope had suffered a mighty defeat.

All my brothers had fled in confusion and fear. However, as they continued to work through their grief, they decided in unison: "We must bid him goodbye!" Bethany was as unsafe as Jerusalem, for the officials knew we camped there often. Returning to Galilee with a failed mission was not an option, either. We would be objects of much banter at Capernaum and Bethsaida; I could picture our townsfolk shaking their heads, pitying us for chasing after the wind. However, our minds numbed, and hearts seized with heaviness, we returned to Jerusalem by sunset on that Sabbath day to bid farewell to Jesus.

We planned to visit Jesus' tomb on the first day after Sabbath with the women, who waited to anoint his body with spices and perfumes. Lazarus and his sisters, Mary and Martha, desired to accompany us. Jesus had been their confidante and a cherished friend. The sisters kept chanting, "He will rise again." I pitied their denial. They had memories only of Jesus' power. I had witnessed him stripped of it.

None of us had slept since the night in the garden. Andrew bid us restore our strength before we journeyed to Jerusalem, but while Jesus rested in his grave, I tossed and turned as I tried to lie down, replaying my hopes and dreams that lay buried with him. Rest evaded me. Had God turned his back on our nation?

23

Jerusalem, The Day after the Sabbath, Passover, 33 AD

It was the first day after the Sabbath; the golden rays from the sun spread through the sky, dispelling the darkness of the night, but failed to dissipate the shadows in my heart. The birds mocked me with their song. Oh, to have the wings of a bird and take to the skies!

Peter and I were in the courtyard of the home of my mother's cousin, where we sought shelter. We deemed it best to visit Jesus' grave one at a time to avoid arousing suspicions of the Roman guards that kept watch there.

While we were deep in thought, Mary of Magdala came storming into the courtyard. Her face was flushed; her was breath short. She was shaking, and her words garbled. As her voice rose and fell, words that I could piece together were *angels, Jesus, missing body,* and then as I observed the movements of her mouth, I could make out the words "He has risen."

My heart nearly stopped.

I took her by her hand and helped her sit. Peter gave her a drink of water. Like us, she had hardly slept. At the break of day, she, along with Jesus' mother Mary, had rushed to Jesus' grave to prepare and anoint his body as per our custom. Of all the women who accompanied us, Mary of Magdala left no stone unturned in serving Jesus, her heart overflowing with love for her redeemer. After all, he had delivered her from seven demons. Since Jesus died, she had not uttered a word until now, when she attempted to narrate the events of that morning.

This is her account:

"As his mother and I approached the cave where his body lay, we saw the stone rolled away. I panicked because the guards were nowhere in sight; we assumed they removed the Teacher's body without telling us. They had robbed us of our right to bid the Teacher an honorable goodbye. Overcome with sorrow, we fell to the ground. At once, we were aware of two men in shining clothes, one on either side of the entrance to the tomb. They exhorted us. 'Why look for the living among the dead?'

Discerning that they were angels, we fell to the ground. They disappeared in a flash. We were unsure of what their words meant. I was determined to complete the burial rituals. I ran inside the cave to search for his body once again. It was then that I saw him. I barely recognized him. Thinking he was the gardener, I begged him to tell us if he knew where they had taken the Teacher.

It was not until he called me by name that I discerned he was the Teacher.

He seemed different. His face was shining, and so was his robe. He bid me instruct you to return to Galilee, where he will go ahead of you."

My hope in Jesus had ebbed and flowed many times. Despair weighed heavy on my soul and prevented me from believing Mary's words right away. She could have imagined it all, driven out of her mind with grief. Jesus' mother Mary had followed Mary of Magdala into the courtyard.

Her face was glowing. Could what Mary of Magdala narrated be true? There was only one way to find out. I dashed to the tomb. I ran like the wind. Peter followed.

Mary had been right about the stone; It was rolled away, and Pretonius and his men were nowhere in sight. It was most unlike a Roman guard, much less a centurion, to abandon his post. My heart skipped a beat as I made my way into the tomb. The spot where Jesus' body lay was vacant save for the strips of burial linen. The burial cloth, used as a head covering, was placed where his head would have been. I was struck by the manner of its fold—without a crease, and each pleat neatly gathered. I froze. I had watched Jesus fold his prayer shawl many times. Was this a dream? I turned around and shouted at Peter. "He is not here!"

Peter bolted into the cave. Upon seeing the empty tomb, he cupped his hands over his mouth and ran out. We rushed back to alert the others.

Back at the house, the others greeted us in disbelief. Mary of Magdala had recounted the events of that morning to them as well.

"Is it true?" Andrew's face was flushed.

"His body is missing," Peter replied.

James groaned. "Our troubles keep multiplying. The authorities will blame this on us!"

I tried to remain calm. "Perhaps, he has risen as he said."

"What proof do you have?" Thomas chimed in.

Mary insisted. "I have seen the Teacher!"

We were afraid to leave the house, fearing the authorities would seek our arrest. My brothers were deep in thought. How could a body disappear from a secure tomb?

~

It was late afternoon when I heard the whinnying of a horse in the courtyard. It was Flavius Marcus. He rode alone. An arrest usually required a unit of at least a dozen men. Peter and I went to meet him in the courtyard.

"If you know where his body is, pray tell me." Flavius implored us. "Petronius tells me a strange tale of an earthquake and beings like lightning who rolled the stone from the entrance of the cave; he is a most trusted centurion, and if he recounts his tale to Pilate, I fear for his head. Please return your teacher's body, and I swear by Jupiter, you will not be harmed!"

It did not take us long to convince Flavius Marcus that we were blameless. Our bewilderment was evident to him. Petronius had also witnessed angels by the tombstone. Flavius believed us; deep within, he always knew that the prophet from Galilee was no ordinary man.

Flavius Marcus left, warning us to flee. "Next time I may have to knock on your door with imperial orders!"

We needed no persuasion. We decided we would seek shelter outside Jerusalem in the home of John Mark, the one who hosted our Passover meal.

Also, Flavius Marcus need not have worried about his men. We learned later that the chief priests and the elders bribed them. "You are to say that his disciples stole his body while we slept; we will make sure the governor does not hold you accountable."

The guards did as our elders desired, and their lives were spared, but the threat to ours increased.

My brothers and I secured the doors and windows, drew the curtains as we sat contemplating the events of that day.

Confusion and despair hung over us even as Mary held on to her story and his mother wept for joy. I could not get my mind off the burial cloth. There was no mistaking its folds; however, two questions remained. Where was Jesus? What next?

As evening set in, the women lit an oil lamp for us and proceeded to assist our host with dinner. Our shadows loomed large on the wall across from me. I started counting them to relieve my mind of its chatter. There were eleven of us now, with Judas gone. I shuddered at the thought of his end. We were ten in the room that evening, for Thomas, had taken off to prepare for our stay at the home of John Mark.

One, two, three, four… ten, eleven.

Eleven? I counted again and again. My eyes, devoid of sleep, were playing tricks. Then a familiar voice said, "Peace be with you!"

We covered our faces with our cloaks, thinking it was a ghost.

Then Jesus spoke again. "Why are you fearful and doubtful? Look, it is I. Touch my hands and feet, for a spirit does not have flesh and bones."

We uncovered our faces and looked up. There, before us, stood Jesus, light pouring from his face, with his hands stretched towards us, with the nail-pierced holes in his palms. Awestruck, we neither spoke nor moved.

Jesus broke the silence. "Do you have anything for me to eat?"

I was bewildered. Could a spirit feel hunger?

That evening, Jesus shared a meal with us. As he broke the bread in the manner he was used to, I could not hold back my tears. I basked in the joy that Jesus lived once more. My heart churned within me as he opened up the scriptures to us, explaining how the Messiah needed to suffer and die. He assured us. "Everything written about me in the books of the laws and prophets needed to be fulfilled." His kingdom was not of this world, as he had proclaimed to Pilate. It would take me a lifetime to grasp his mission. While we were still eating, Jesus vanished from our midst.

Thomas was in disbelief when he returned. "I must place my hands in his scars and see for myself!"

And Jesus granted his wish. He appeared a week later to Thomas and permitted him to touch his body and place his fingers in the holes in his hands and feet. Thomas fell at Jesus' feet and wept. Jesus said, "Blessed are they who have not seen and yet believed."

I was eager to share our witness about his resurrection. Knowing my thoughts, Jesus cautioned us to wait until we received power from heaven.

Then he vanished once more. We knew what we had to do next. He instructed us to return to Galilee, where he would meet us again. We canceled our plans to hide in the home of John Mark in the upper room and journeyed back to Galilee. The women, too, accompanied us.

And thus, once again, we returned to the sea.

24

Galilee, 33 AD

Once home, the sea welcomed us with open arms. Our townsfolk did not. However, their disbelief and disdain could not dampen my excitement. I was pregnant with hope once more. What did Jesus have in store for us? How long should we wait for him? What were we to do in the meantime?

My brothers and I thought it best to take to the sea. This time we were not four, but eleven as the others joined us. Peter's wife and mother-in-law were gracious hosts, and the sea brought cheer to my heart. My brothers marveled when I taught them to catch fish with bare hands. However, we were not so fortunate with our nets as the fish refused to bite during the day. We hoped to get them at night.

On the third night, James, Peter, Andrew, Nathaniel, Thomas, and I ventured out on the sea hoping it would deliver its bounty, but alas, no fish.

No Jesus, either.

Sleepless, exhausted, and hungry, we were about to pull our boats ashore when, in the light of the rising sun, we saw from afar the figure of a man.

"Friends, do you have any fish?" he asked.

"No!" we replied.

"Throw your net on the right side of the boat; you will find some."

I turned my back to my brothers and stared at the man on the shore. I let out a scream. "It is the Lord, Peter!" Before I could turn around, there was a splash. Peter had jumped into the water and was walking to the shore. Sure enough, when we drew our net, the boat was full. We counted a hundred and fifty-three fish later that day. Thomas and Nathaniel rushed back to get the others while Andrew, James, and I towed the net.

None of us spoke. We knew it was the Lord, though his appearance was different—bright as the noonday sun.

Jesus smiled. He had a fire going. He pointed to the burning coal with bread and fish on it. "Go get some more of the fish you have caught. Let us share a meal."

I will always cherish the memory of that breakfast by the sea. Oh, what a comfort to have Jesus with us again!

Breakfast turned into lunch as we communed. Unable to help myself, I burst out, "Teacher, will you establish the kingdom promised to us by God?"

"Be assured! Your Father in heaven will surely fulfill his word! As for His kingdom, it is here already." And then Jesus opened our scriptures for us. Beginning with Moses and the law, he walked us through the scrolls of our prophets and enlightened us about every writing concerning himself, the Messiah, the promised one, and why he had to suffer and die. We marveled as he quoted every word from memory without the scrolls. Our hearts burned within us as our minds were enlightened.

It was incredible to witness Jesus more alive and real than he had ever been. Not even his transfiguration on the mountain could compare. He had come back from the dead, yet, unlike Lazarus, whom he raised from the dead, Jesus could walk through walls and transport himself anywhere in an instant. Yet, he was not a ghost. He was from another world as he had said to Pilate—"My kingdom is not of this world!"

As he continued to shine a light in our minds regarding his kingdom, this world, this life, and the afterlife, something in me stirred. I sensed he would not be with us forever. A tinge of sadness pricked my heart.

That afternoon, Jesus vanished from our sight in a flash, just as he had appeared, assuring us he would return. There was much he needed to teach us, and he bid us return to Jerusalem.

The Shavuot festival was a week in progress in the holy city. It is a celebration of the harvest and culminates seven weeks after the Passover. We sent word to Lazarus, Mary, and Martha to receive us, which they were eager to do.

Peter, Andrew, and the others headed to prepare for our journey back to Judea. I took off to the synagogue to request a set of blank scrolls from the scribes. The last time I wrote on one was as a teenager eager to please my teachers with the practice of scribing our laws from memory at the school. It was time to record again—not the law, but Jesus' words.

That day, Jesus had opened our minds apart from our traditions, his teaching based on a radical notion—"The dwelling of God is with man, not in a temple shaped by hands." He unlocked the book of our law (Leviticus) and the Prophets. "My dwelling place shall be with them, and I will be their God, and they shall be my people."

Jesus had alluded to it when he lived as one of us, but our minds, beholden to our customs, were darkened, unable to comprehend. We failed to understand the sign from heaven—the veil in the holy sanctuary ripped apart when Jesus gave up his spirit. He was the bridge between our world and his, in the bosom of his Father above. This message would become a raging fire and consume us, even to the point of laying down our lives.

His words continue to ring in my ears—"The old order is passing away." No more atonement sacrifices or burnt offerings, or temple rituals. No more slaughter of the innocent—another Abel need never shed his blood! I heaved a sigh of relief.

Jesus bid us search within for the laws of God inscribed upon our hearts, not on tablets of stone that were handed to us by Moses. Would our people accept it? Would my father agree? Our leaders and rabbis were sure to object. Jesus warned us several times, even when he was alive. "They rejected me; they will reject you! They will cast you out and consider it a service to God but do not lose heart. My Father will send you a helper from above!"

Who could this helper be? Was it the warring archangel Michael or the messenger of God, Gabriel?

My brothers and I mused over Jesus' teachings that night. Do we place our faith in our centuries-old traditions and laws, the legacy we so carefully guarded, or in the one that came to us from heaven in the flesh, who overcame the grave and appeared to us clothed in the glory that can be due only to God?

While I lay in bed mulling over these questions, a cloud lifted from my mind. I bolted out of bed and grabbed my scrolls. I scribed these words on it: The word became flesh and made his dwelling among us. We have seen his glory, the glory of the one and only Son, who came from the Father, full of grace and truth. No one has ever seen God, but the one and only Son has made him known. The light shines in the darkness, and the darkness has not overcome it.

25

Judea, Bethany, 33 AD

"Has he risen as he said he would?" Mary, Lazarus' sister, burst out upon seeing us at the door. I grinned. "You were always one to heed his words carefully, Mary. It is as you say!"

The color rose in Mary's cheeks, and she rushed to get Lazarus and Martha. We were weary from our travels but could not wait to share our excitement with our hosts. We recounted all the events of Jesus' resurrection, and how he taught us by the sea.

While we were gathered at dinner that night, Jesus appeared once again. I leaned forward to lay my head on his bosom as was my habit but then drew back. A holy radiance emanated from him. I covered my face in reverence. Jesus held out his hand and bid me to his side. "You are one with me, John!"

"The words you speak are hard for us and difficult to understand, teacher!"

"I have much more to say to you, but indeed it is hard for you to grasp. When the helper comes, he will illuminate my words and guide you in the truth I now speak to you. He will comfort you and lead you to the Father's heart, and as I am in the Father and the Father is in me, you too will be in me and I in you."

His words puzzled us. No one spoke. Even Peter, who was usually quick to speak, remained silent. I voiced what we were thinking, "Who is the helper, and by what sign shall we recognize him?"

Jesus' eyes softened, and he placed his hand on my shoulder. "By fire from heaven, John. Isn't that what you have desired? I will not leave you as orphans. I, myself, will come to you. You shall know me as wind and fire!"

While I was scratching my head over his words, at last, Andrew spoke. "Will you establish us as a nation when you return to us? What about the kingdom of God?

"For sure, your Father in heaven will fulfill his promise to his people, but it is not given to us to know the times and the season when that comes about; as for God's kingdom, it is here already. Do you not perceive it? The lame walk, the blind see, and the dead are raised to life. You will be my witnesses bearing this message: The Lord your God dwells in you, and you shall no longer seek him in a temple made by human hands or come before Him in fear. The blood of the messiah has forever replaced the slaughter of innocent bulls, goats, and lambs, releasing you from the weight of the harsh judgments of the laws!"

The room broke out in chatter. "But Lord," Peter chimed in, "those who opposed you seek our lives. If we teach, as you say, they will surely put an end to us all." Before Jesus could answer him, Matthew spoke up. "How can we oppose God and Moses, to whom He gave our laws?"

James jumped in as well. "What about our forefathers? Shall we dishonor their legacy?"

Mary, sister of Lazarus, too, implored Jesus. "Lord, the authorities are making sure that your resurrection is passed off, as deception. How then will anyone believe in us and the message you have given us?"

At this, Jesus stood up and bid us all be at peace. "Remain in Jerusalem and do not leave the city until you receive help from above. Your heavenly Father will clothe you with power from the highest realms, and the helper, when he comes, will equip you with strength and the right words. When you are arrested before authorities and wonder what to speak, the helper will give you utterances and enable you to do greater works and miracles than what I have performed amongst you. Do not let your hearts be fearful!"

We remained in Bethany for some time, and Jesus appeared to us several times over the next forty days from his resurrection, teaching, and communing with us.

And then the day came for him to ascend to his Father. The eleven of us, his mother Mary, Mary of Magdala and Lazarus, and his sisters, followed him to the wilderness outside of Bethany. Here he lifted his hands, blessed us, and let out a loud breath, bestowing his life force upon us while we bowed down in worship. When we looked up, he had begun his ascent towards the skies.

A giant pit appeared in my stomach, pressed into my chest, working its way to a lump in my throat. Would Jesus leave us yet again?

While I stood there, my head hung low and my heart crushed with sorrow once more, I heard Jesus say, "I will be with you till the end of the ages." Then a giant cloud hid him from our sight; at once, two men clad in white stood beside us and comforted us. "Men of Galilee," they said, "why do you stand here looking into the sky? This same Jesus, who has ascended to heaven, will come back in the same way you have seen him depart."

Strengthened by this assurance, we departed to Jerusalem, to the house of John Mark. While we waited for the helper to arrive, we committed ourselves to remain in union with each other and God, as Jesus had taught us.

Although Jesus appeared to several others after his resurrection, no one dared declare it for fear of being cast out of their synagogues and temples. Our temple leaders were confident of having succeeded in their endeavor to crush any reports of Jesus rising from the dead. Seeing that we were no longer a threat, they dropped their efforts to arrest us.

Meanwhile, to replace Judas' bitter memory, we cast lots to decide who we could add to our mission as witnesses of Jesus' resurrection and message. The lot fell on one named Mathias, and we were twelve once again. We waited for the helper. He arrived on the last day of the festival, the fiftieth day after the Passover.

And bridged the divide between heaven and earth.

26

Jerusalem, 33 AD

We gathered in the upper room once again—the same one where we had celebrated our last Passover with Jesus. Men and women in and around Jerusalem who had witnessed the resurrection joined us. Their number was a hundred and twenty. They had been fearful of the authorities, but once they found out we were in the city, they were eager to share their experience of the risen Jesus. Amidst them were two disciples from the town of Emmaus who had shared their evening meal with the resurrected Jesus and could not wait to recount their experience to us.

We had surprising company as well—Jesus' brothers. For the risen Jesus appeared to them, his acceptance and forgiveness melting their stony hearts. The 'prophet had gained honor in his hometown' at last. Jesus' brother, James, was eager to embark upon the mission that Jesus had entrusted us. But he, too, would have to wait for the helper to arrive.

It was the day of Pentecost, the fiftieth day from the Passover. We were all gathered in that upper story when there was a roar from heaven, a mighty rushing wind that encircled us, and tongues of fire appeared and rested on each one of us, sparks everywhere.

Whenever Mother had recounted the story of Moses' first encounter with God in a fiery bush, I had marveled how it might have been ablaze and not destroyed. Until that day when the helper descended on us. We were the burning bush—enveloped in flames but not consumed.

As the fire circled us, the words of the baptizer, John, when he had first pointed to Jesus, came to mind: "I baptize you with water, but he will baptize you with Spirit and fire!"

An ocean of peace engulfed me. The presence of Jesus, his kindness and gentleness, was unmistakable. He had returned to us as he promised, albeit not in the flesh. For the helper was none other than Jesus, not the teacher or prophet, but the life force, the presence of God—not only with us but now in us!

I lifted my hands and opened my mouth to praise the Lord our God and could not understand the words I uttered, for I spoke in a tongue I could not discern. My body was like a feather floating, outside the bounds of time. The words poured forth like a fountain, making their way from my belly and out of my mouth. Is this what Jesus had spoken to the Samaritan woman? "He who believes in me shall never thirst; out of his belly shall flow streams of living waters."

And my brothers and all who had gathered there shared in this experience. The roar from heaven and the sound of our prayers in various tongues drew a large crowd to the house. The city was bursting with pilgrims from different cities— Parthians, Medes, Elamites, Mesopotamians, Judeans, Arabs, Cretans, Cappadocians, and those from Phrygia, Pamphylia, Pontus, Egypt, and the areas of Libya around Cyrene, and Rome. Each one of our neighbors and those who were passing by heard us speaking in their native languages. Some wondered, "Are not these disciples of Jesus from Galilee? How is it that we each hear them in our tongue?" Others were not impressed. "These men are drunk and without sense!"

At this accusation, Peter stood before the crowd that had gathered outside the house. His face shining as if anointed with oil, and his eyes beaming, he addressed them with boldness and calmness that had taken hold of him: "It is only nine in the morning. It is too early for anyone to be drunk. What you perceive is the fulfillment of God's words as he spoke to through our prophets in times past, fulfilled through his son Jesus whom you handed over for crucifixion, but God has raised him from the dead and placed him in authority over heaven and earth. All this happened to fulfill God's desire that we may no longer rely upon priests and sacrifices but believe in Jesus' authority to forgive our trespasses and receive the gift of God's Spirit and communion with the Father who had been veiled in our temple and shrouded with laws and rituals. He has poured his Spirit on us, and now, he will pour it on all men, women, young and old alike, so that they may enter his presence freely. This is the kingdom of God that Jesus spoke of while he taught amongst you, a message of which we have become custodians."

All who heard Peter were amazed. "Is this not the unlearned fisherman from Galilee? Look how he speaks, and we hear him in our language!"

The number of people that believed in Peter's message that day was three thousand. They followed us to the Jordan River, requesting baptism into the new way of life. It was an affair that lasted several hours. We neither ate bread nor drank water, energized by the Spirit, and an unspeakable joy reverberated through the fabric of our being. So, this is how

Jesus ministered all day without food or drink! He had often said, "My food is to do my Father's work."

That night, we gathered in the upper room once again, exhausted, yet refreshed. The room was humming with excited chatter. Andrew stood in our midst and addressed us. "Brothers and sisters, it is not a coincidence that we baptized three thousand men and women on this day!"

Matthew was quick to pick up on Andrew's cue. "Today, we commemorate the day when Moses received the law on Mount Sinai. The number of our forefathers that disobeyed the law and perished by fire at the foot of the mountain that day was three thousand."

"Exactly!" Andrew's face shone as he continued, and it is on this day that the fire which has fallen on us has removed the sting of the law that Moses handed to us."

A veil lifted from my mind. On one of the blank scrolls that I carried in my satchel, I quickly scribed these words: The law was given through Moses, but grace and truth came through Jesus Christ.

The next day, I was awakened by the first rays of the sun streaming in through a large window across from where I lay. The room was quiet except for Peter's gentle snores. I smiled as my gaze fell on him. His boldness had been contagious. Who would have thought that a few days prior, he feared being identified as a disciple of Jesus?

I tip-toed towards the window. The birds were chirping in song. My heart, too, was bursting with a new tune—the melody of good news. The God of our forefathers, so far removed from us by laws and rituals, in whose presence priests and prophets trembled, had broken all barriers that separate man from his maker and wrapped his creation in an affectionate and everlasting embrace.

A truth unveiled, a different way of life, and we were beacons of it.

As I watched the world beneath the window, lying in stillness, I smiled. While it lay in deep slumber, a new era dawned upon it.

27

Jerusalem, 33 AD

The day after the Pentecost, we bid goodbye to several new brothers and sisters. These men and women joined caravans of pilgrims returning to their towns and cities, eager to take the words of Jesus with them. In a few short days, we had become a family, united by one spirit and one purpose—to share the good news of Jesus' resurrection and the outpouring of God's presence within us.

The twelve of us, including Matthias, who replaced Judas, along with Jesus' mother and brothers, Lazarus and his sisters, and Mary from Magdala, remained in that upper room and contemplated our next move. Looking out the window, I glimpsed the smoke rising from the temple. The afternoon sacrifice was in progress. I motioned to Peter, "Shall we go to the temple? Many will be there at this time. Perhaps some may receive our message?"

Peter jumped at my suggestion, his face beaming. The presence of the helper and the conversion of the three thousand had lit a spark in us. The fire from heaven had consumed our fears. The change was most evident in Peter, for he forgave Matthew.

We hurried to the temple to share Jesus' message with any who were willing to listen. On the way, we saw a man, lame from birth, being carried to the temple gate where it was his custom to beg from the worshippers. He stretched out his hands and opened his palm as we entered the temple. We looked straight at him, and Peter commanded him. "Look at us!" As the man cast an expectant gaze on us, Peter continued, "I do not have silver or gold to give you, but what I do have, I give you. In the name of Jesus who rose from the dead, walk."

Then, taking him by the right hand, Peter helped him up. At once, the man's feet and ankles gained strength. He jumped to his feet and leaped into the temple courts, shouting praises to God. All, who knew he was crippled from the womb, were struck with wonder and amazement. The man clung to Peter and me, falling at our feet with tears of joy.

A large crowd came running towards us, their eyes wide open and mouths gaping. Peter addressed them in a loud voice. "My fellow men, why does this surprise you? Why do you stare at us as if, by our power or godliness, we had made this man walk? The God of our fathers has glorified his servant Jesus. You disowned him before Pilate, condemned the author of life to death, but God raised him from the dead. We are witnesses to this. Jesus' name has completely healed this man, as you can all see. He is the one of whom Moses spoke and said: "the Lord your God will raise for you a prophet like me from among your people; you must listen to everything he tells you."

In the books of our laws, Moses established for us, who were conscience-stricken, a way of redemption through sacrifices, feasts, and rituals. Yet these, though performed day after day, year after year, brought us no peace. Jesus has cleansed our conscience once and for all. We may enter a time of refreshing and rest in the Lord our God, who longs to dwell with and within you, not in a temple made by human hands! This gift of God is not only for us but for all the inhabitants of this world."

The hair on the back of my neck stood tall as I heard Peter speak. For it was not Peter, but Jesus who was moving in and through him with the words which he had spoken to the Samaritan woman at Jacob's well: "a time is coming when the Father will seek those who worship not on Mount Gerizim or Jerusalem, but in spirit and truth."

Many placed their trust in Peter's words and the miracle they witnessed that day, muttering amongst themselves. "Surely, we crucified a godly man; look how he lives and moves through his disciples. Could these men be right? Where did they get such authority and boldness to speak about our laws and prophets?"

But others feared the temple leaders and desired to remain in their favor and rushed off to report to them. "His disciples are at the temple perpetuating deception and false teachings against Moses!"

The priests and the captain of the temple guards rushed to refrain Peter and me from speaking to the people. They were agitated because we proclaimed Jesus resurrected from the dead. They arrested us for a trial before the Sanhedrin the following day. All this time, we had been fearful of being thrown in prison. When it finally happened, we found ourselves jubilant and celebrating, for a host of men and women, numbering two thousand, believed in our message that day.

The next day the elders and teachers of the law, Annas the high priest, and Caiaphas confronted us. "By whose authority did you heal the lame man?"

Then Peter, overflowing with the Holy Spirit, answered them: "Rulers and elders of the people! If we are held accountable today for an act of kindness shown to a man who was lame and questioned how we healed him, then know this that it is by the name of Jesus of Nazareth, whom you crucified but whom God raised from the dead, that this man stands before you healed."

The rulers were astounded both by our courage and by the miracle, for they knew we were ordinary men, and yet the lame man crippled for over forty years stood beside us healed. Not wanting to draw the attention of the masses, they ordered us to withdraw and threatened us lest we speak to anyone in the name of Jesus.

But Peter and I remained undeterred. I knew not what came over us. We challenged them. "Which is right in God's eyes: to listen to you, or God? We cannot help proclaiming that which we have witnessed."

They continued to threaten us. Nicodemus and another teacher, Gamaliel, rose from among the rulers and assured them. "It is best to leave these men alone; if they are lawbreakers, God will surely be their judge! But if what they say and do is from God, you will find yourselves fighting against God!"

At this, the Sanhedrin let us go, forbidding us to proclaim Jesus' resurrection or teach and heal in his name.

But we were just getting started.

When we returned to the upper room, we found the others anxious and excited. News of the lame man had reached them, and they were relieved at our acquittal. However, Andrew wondered if it was safe for us to remain in the city much longer.

Andrew's concern was not unfounded. That night, as we rested after dinner, the sound of hooves outside our window caught our attention. It was Flavius Marcus. He was looking over his shoulder as he rode through the narrow path leading up to the house. His helmet and sword were by his side.

"I come in peace," he said, laying his sword at our feet. "Make haste to leave Jerusalem, for your priests and elders have conspired with Pilate and the Herodians to charge and arrest you for treason!"

We spoke in unison. "What are the charges against us?"

"Have you been proclaiming that the teacher rose from the dead and that he is the son of God? Caesar Augustus has exalted himself as the son of our God Apollo. Anyone who regards another as the son of God is a traitor! Your authorities plan to hand you over to Rome, as they did your teacher. Hurry and leave Jerusalem before I have to march against you!" He bowed his head and knelt before us. "Please do not let your blood be on my hands!"

I marveled at the Roman official, the commander of legions, who bowed before Jewish men for the sake of Jewish blood.

We took heed of Flavius Marcus' warning and departed for Galilee that night. John Mark accompanied us, and so did Jesus' mother and brothers. Lazarus and his sisters made their way to Bethany.

We were on the run once again. And then it dawned on me—our struggle was no longer against a foreign oppressor.

We were at war with our own nation.

28

Galilee, 33 AD

Banished from the temple in Jerusalem with the warning from Flavius Marcus ringing fresh in our ears, Peter, Andrew, James, and I returned to the sea. The others made their way to their respective homes. Father was relieved to have us back; it had become increasingly difficult for him to be the sole overseer of our enterprise, which had increased while we were away. He had bought new boats and hired more men, but none that could replace us.

But neither my family nor the sea could bring rest to my heart. The instructions of Jesus were like a fire raging in my bones: "Heal the sick, raise the dead, tell the people the Messiah is the lamb slain at the altar for their trespasses once and for all, the kingdom of God is with man."

While we were out at sea, James and I shared this message with all the fishermen who were willing to listen. Andrew and Peter spent each Sabbath teaching the masses at the synagogue in Capernaum. The scribes and Pharisees, who had taught us, who deemed Andrew as a treasured student, threw their hands up in the air. "We failed to train you well!"

However, Peter bewildered them. "Is this not the one who loitered the streets while we taught his brothers? He is unschooled in our laws, yet he speaks about Moses and the Messiah with such authority!"

They wondered amongst themselves. "What has gotten into these men?" However, they did not thirst for our blood, as did the leaders in Jerusalem.

Meanwhile, the zealots in Galilee expressed their disappointment. "We placed our trust in Jesus to deliver us from Rome!"

"Rome is not your enemy!" I could hardly believe the words that poured forth from my lips.

"Then who is?"

And just like that, without a thought, the words gushed out of my mouth. "We are our enemy."

At this, the Zealots left, shaking their heads, muttering with pity. "He has been driven to insanity!"

That night, as I lay in bed, I marveled at the words I had spoken earlier. My sleep was deep, and my dreams scattered: Little, innocent Abel scampering away from the altar of his sacrifice, the leaders in Jerusalem admonishing us, Father's face beaming with joy at our arrival, the flash of the Roman sword, not stained with blood but laid at my feet, Flavius Marcus kneeling before me.

I sat upright on my bed. I was no longer a slave to the yearning that held me captive all these years—the cords of bitterness and revenge which bound me to Rome had been severed; the guilt of Abel's blood was lifted. My heart leaped with the stride of a man set free from prison—that of his mind.

Our prophet Isaiah's words that Jesus had quoted during our first visit to his hometown came to remembrance: "The spirit of the Lord has anointed me to preach good news to the poor, to open the eyes that are blind… to set the captives free." And we were to bear this message of freedom to the ends of the earth, as Jesus had instructed. For that, we had to leave Galilee. I rushed to consult with Andrew.

The next day, I found Andrew and Peter by the seashore, cleaning the boat. I implored them.

"We should return to Jerusalem and gather all the brothers. There are many disciples there who have witnessed Jesus' resurrection. They can help us spread the message that Jesus has entrusted us, and it must reach the farthest corners of the empire!"

"And beyond, John!" Andrew's eyes were gleaming.

Peter nodded. "He wanted us to catch men, not just fish!"

But this time, our families were apprehensive.

Mother wept. She reasoned with us. "Can you not teach in the synagogue here? Must you provoke the authorities? They will hand you over to Rome or stone you to death. Why not gather all your brothers and preach in all the towns of Galilee?"

Father worried he would be banished from the temple or incur the displeasure of our God. "I believe in the Messiah, but we cannot forget Moses. Our laws are the pride of our nation, and the temple is its crown. Your message goes against Moses!"

We failed to persuade Father that Jesus held out a better hope for our people, a new covenant with our God, where serving the laws of Moses was no longer a mandate. He shook his head as he bid us goodbye the next day.

We set off for Jerusalem, not knowing what awaited us. We trusted the Helper would guide us. My heart was full as I recalled Jesus' exhortation—"You will be my witnesses to the ends of the earth."

29

Judea, 34 AD

We gained a large following in and around Jerusalem, despite the hostility of our leaders. Many placed their faith in Jesus' resurrection, believing he was the Messiah, one greater than Moses. We banded together, sharing our belongings, and guarding each other's interests as our own. We were united in purpose and prayed and broke bread together.

It was the first Passover since Jesus rose from the dead. We were no longer twelve but over several hundred. It was my first Passover without a lamb. As we gathered once more in that upper room and partook of the cup, I recalled the day Jesus bled, each drop of his blood erasing every letter of the law that kept us trapped in fear of God. If only our leaders would believe in the one greater than the prophets, they, too, would be free from the yoke of the laws and harsh judgments laid on us by our forefathers.

But it was not just the love of Moses that kept them glued to their seats in the temple. It was love for the seat itself.

Meanwhile, as we twelve devoted ourselves to prayer and teaching, we appointed seven men who could help us minister to the needs of the ever-increasing number of disciples added to our congregation daily. We chose these seven men to minister to the needs of the crowd who followed us: Stephen, a wise man filled with the Holy Spirit; Philip, Prochorus, Nicanor, Timon, Parmenas, and Nicolaus from Antioch, a gentile who observed and favored the Jewish traditions.

Armed with strength and support from new believers, our zeal to teach the ways of Jesus knew no bounds. The Spirit of Jesus radiated through us all, manifesting miracle upon miracle—the greatest of them, the conversion of stony hearts, for many priests from the temple joined our cause.

Our prophets had pointed to this day, though none of us understood until Jesus rose from the dead, and we received the Helper, the Holy Spirit. The promise of God, delivered through our prophet Joel, was fulfilled: "I will pour my Spirit upon all flesh."

As our faith grew, so did our troubles. The conversion of some of the temple priests sparked much anger and protest. Saul, a Pharisee from Tarsus in the Roman province of Asia Minor, was in Jerusalem for the Passover. He had heard of Jesus and of our work to convert the hearts of our people to the Messiah. So zealous was he for the ways of our forefathers that he had Stephen captured and brought before the Sanhedrin. Stephen remained undeterred during his interrogation, proclaiming Jesus as the Messiah. He stood facing the temple authorities, his face shining. "Jesus is the one of whom Moses had spoken of and said, 'God will raise another, you must listen to him.'"

Infuriated by Stephen's claim, Saul thundered. "Have the followers of the way deceived you too?" We were known as 'the way' that betrayed our nation and opposed God.

Stephen did not defend himself. Instead, he challenged the authorities with their scriptures, beginning with God's covenant with Abraham, the father of our nation, and ending with Moses and the prophets who foretold the coming of Jesus.

Outraged by his boldness, the Sanhedrin charged him as they had Jesus. "This man is a blasphemer." They pelted him with stones.

And once again, I watched pricked in my heart as I witnessed Stephen fall to the ground slathered in blood. He gathered himself, lifted his hands to heaven, and declared, "I see Jesus at the right hand of God on the clouds!" His bold claim fueled the flames of anger that burned against him, and the teachers at the temple hurled larger stones at him.

As Stephen sensed his time to depart this world, draw near, he prayed. "Lord Jesus, forgive these men for they do not know what they are doing!"

Stephen turned towards Saul as he spoke. Saul was standing at a distance, guarding the possessions of the men driven by blood lust to satisfy the law that demanded Stephen's death. As Stephen's gaze met his, I noticed him falter. His eyes, hard as steel, softened, albeit momentarily. Then Stephen cried out in a loud voice. "Lord Jesus, receive my spirit!"

Stephen had never seen Jesus in the flesh nor encountered the risen Christ as we had, but in the short time he was with us, he lived and died like Jesus, forgiving those who persecuted him. Jesus' words rang true: "They will consider killing you an offering to God."

I mourned Stephen's death long after we buried him. My heart, though heavy, welled with pride. Stephen could have called down fire and plagues on those who opposed us, for the power of God was in him as it was in Jesus. Any of my brothers or I could have done that.

But we did not.

The fire that fell on us from heaven burned in us as compassion for our oppressors. I pitied those who hurled stones at Stephen, for there is no oppression greater than the power of the law and a conscience subservient to it.

Of all those who opposed us, there was none more formidable than Saul of Tarsus. His zeal to hunt and kill us surpassed that of the Pharisees in Jerusalem. He went from door to door where there was the slightest hint of a gathering of the followers of the way and had our brothers and sisters arrested. Saul resolved to secure orders from the high priest in Jerusalem for the synagogues in the large cities like Damascus to apprehend any who were our disciples and have them tried in Jerusalem. Saul swore not to rest until the last one of us was silenced, either through surrender or execution.

We fled Jerusalem, each of us scattered through various towns and cities of Galilee, Judea, and into the Syrian provinces of the empire. We bore no sword save for the sword of truth, the truth that pierced the hearts of our leaders and invoked their envy and rage. I left Jesus' mother in the care of Mary from Magdala and my mother, who was lodging with her cousin in Jerusalem and took off to Samaria with Peter. The town of Sychar, where Jesus had taught the woman at Jacob's well, welcomed us—a respite from our struggles in Jerusalem.

I hoped never to encounter Saul again.

Fourteen years later, we stood face to face in Jerusalem.

30

It had been four years since Jesus rose from the dead. Our message was spreading like wildfire, adding to the number of our friends and foes. Meanwhile, our nation was a boiling pot. The Zealots banded together from across the Jewish provinces but were no match for the Roman armies. However, each blood bath only fueled the Zealots' demand for autonomy. Governor Pilate failed to contain these revolts, and Caiaphas fared no better. These political predicaments were the least of their troubles. We, the disciples of Jesus, proved to be more than just a thorn in their side.

The report of a risen Messiah, the Son of God, a savior from heaven, spread throughout the empire, provoking the emperor's fury. The Roman emperor alone reserved the rights to the title, Son of God, to whom homage was due. The message of Jesus posed yet another dilemma for the Roman rulers who had been tolerant of our Jewish practices and customs thus far. Many high-ranking Roman officials like Cornelius, a reputed centurion, along with his family and some members of Pilate's household, believed Jesus was the son of the divine. Our message also diffused through higher ranks of the Roman military because of the testimony of Flavius Marcus. Hundreds of Greeks and Romans placed their confidence in our message—one cannot find rest in this life or the afterlife by pleasing the gods but by faith alone.

The emperor, Tiberius, was alarmed. Rejection of the gods would lead to disregard for the throne and the emperor whom the gods had chosen. Besides, the temples, which were Rome's pride, would be rendered worthless without worshippers. Tiberius commissioned Pilate to crush the mystery cult, yet another label given to us.

But Pontius Pilate was unable to crush our movement, giving rise to a host of rumors — "he conspires with the members of the mystery cult; his wife and household favor them." Tiberius replaced Pilate with Marullus. Pilate was killed while in exile. Whether by his own hand, we do not know. Tiberius, too, was assassinated by the orders of his successor Caligula, one of an unhinged disposition. Caligula preoccupied himself with getting rid of his enemies and had little time to bother with the mystery cult of the Jews. Caiaphas was also duly removed from office for his failure to silence us. His brother-in-law Jonathon was swift to grab his empty seat.

While the southern province of Judea was riddled with political unrest, in the northern province of Galilee, Herod Antipas was busy dealing with conspiracies against him from within his household. Therefore, all eyes were off us for a time, a short but much-needed respite.

Seizing this opportunity, Peter and I, having established congregations of disciples in Samaria, returned to Jerusalem. We were elated to learn how far and wide our brothers had traveled with the words of Jesus—James went to the western borders of Rome, Philip to the South, and Thomas and Andrew to the eastern Roman provinces.

Signs and miracles followed us everywhere, and we recalled Jesus' words with marvel: "You shall do greater works than me."

Now, back in Jerusalem, the greatest wonder awaited us— Saul of Tarsus had a change of heart, zealously proclaiming the same words of Jesus for which he persecuted and killed our brothers.

News of Saul's encounter with the risen Jesus had spread amidst all the disciples in various cities and towns. I shuddered as I recalled those eyes of steel and the heart of stone that stood party to Stephen's murder.

Bright light from heaven had blinded Saul on his way to Damascus, where he bore orders to arrest all the disciples soon after Stephen's death. In Saul's words: "I fell to the ground as the bright light flashed around me. 'Who are you, Lord?' I asked. Then a voice called out to me, 'I am Jesus whom you are persecuting.' Thereafter, I went to the city as Jesus bid me, remained blind for three days, and partook of neither food nor drink. One called Ananias, from among the disciples, prayed for me and my sight was restored. My mind, too, was filled with light. My heart churned within me because I understood Jesus to be the fulfillment of our laws and scriptures and am now zealous to bear his message to all the Gentiles across the empire as Jesus has commissioned me."

So great had been Saul's fury against us that I, along with several disciples, perceived his narrative as a trap.

Until Lazarus brought Barnabas to us.

Barnabas was a faithful disciple and the cousin of John Mark. Barnabas bore witness to Saul's journey and the troubles Saul faced at the hands of the Jewish leaders who sought his life, just as he had once sought ours. Peter was inclined to extend grace towards Saul. His defense- "I fervently denied Jesus, too, didn't I?"

Peter spent fifteen days alone with Saul and James, Jesus' brother, also trusted Saul after meeting him. I learned little about that meeting except that Peter was pleased to have Saul join our cause and said, "Our Lord and teacher has chosen Saul to be a light to the Gentiles just as he has chosen us to be a light to our Jewish brothers."

Thus, Saul left Judea and headed for the province of Syria. It would be another eleven years before I would meet him face to face.

For the next four years, we enjoyed a time of peace. I spent my days in Jerusalem encouraging and building the congregation there, all the while rejecting father's pleas, 'come home' while heeding mother's concern, 'be safe.'

But alas, safety was a child's dream, and our respite was short-lived.

41-43 AD

Herod Antipas' nephew, Agrippa I, accused him of conspiring against the emperor, Caligula. Caligula sent Antipas to exile, and rewarded Agrippa with the title King of the Jews, appointing him ruler over Galilee and Judea. Judea had long been under Roman procurators, and Herod Agrippa was eager to prove his mettle as a Jewish king over the unified provinces. It behooved him to ally with Caiaphas, who did not need his robes to wield command over the people. Thereafter, Agrippa sought to eradicate all the enemies of the Jewish nation, including the disciples of Jesus.

Seeing that it pleased our leaders, Herod Agrippa persecuted us with fervor greater than any of his predecessors.

Amidst the oppression, I experienced an unexpected loss. With help from Jesus' brothers, I laid Mary, mother of Jesus, to rest. That was the beginning of my sorrows.

Soon after, my world fell apart.

44 AD

Armed with the powers of Herod's men, our leaders carried out an organized 'mass purging' against all followers of Jesus. They spilled our blood without mercy. The Herodian soldiers gathered several of the disciples and made a spectacle of their execution. We sought shelter in different towns, strengthening the disciples wherever we went. I had barely recovered from grieving the loss of countless brothers and sisters when I was consumed by anguish, yet again.

James, too, fell to the Herodian sword. As far back as I remembered, it was a Roman sword that haunted me, but in the end, it was my nation's sword that struck my soul.

No food or drink touched my lips for several days. Father, too, died of a broken heart. If only we had heeded his pleas! Mother could not bear this loss alone. James' widow had a little girl to raise. It fell upon me to be the man of the family, but alas, Father was not there to witness it.

There was only one thing left for me to do. I made haste to return to Galilee, to the sea. But the sea would never be the same without my brother.

As the years passed by, the pit in my soul deepened. Darkness crushed my mind. Was spreading Jesus' message worth all this blood?

I went about my days going through the motions of fishing, cleaning boats and nets, eating, and sleeping. I looked to the sea for comfort, but it betrayed me, for its waters carried the imprint of James and Father.

I lost my mission to spread the message of Jesus. I would have lost my will to live if it were not for James' daughter, Aliza. She needed a father, and I needed a reason to get out of bed every morning. There was yet another force to reckon with. Despite the heaviness in my heart, the message of Jesus glowed in it as smoldering embers.

Saul would prove to be my kindling.

31

Jerusalem, 48 AD

As I approached the city gates, my steps were heavy. The city of our God, the city of our forefathers, drunk with the blood of my brothers, lay parched. Smoke from the afternoon sacrifice rose in the distance, a wisp only, not the usual thick pillar. The temple courts were empty save for a few worshippers.

I took care with each step lest the earth beneath my feet should crumble. Giant cracks marred the ground. The fig trees had withered at their roots. The olive trees were downcast, albeit holding on to life. Clouds of despair replaced the rain clouds, hiding the face of heaven.

I slipped my hand into my bag and reached for my purse. The synagogue in Capernaum had shown mercy. I could not wait to bring their collections to my brothers in the city where a new enemy had raised its head—drought and hunger.

I held Peter and Andrew in a long embrace. The last four years were as four hundred. Andrew, Peter, and James, Jesus' brother, had labored in Jerusalem to sustain those who had faced the fires of Agrippa's fury. Peter and Andrew had sold their share of our fishing business and moved their family to Jerusalem to oversee the ever-growing congregation of disciples there.

Herod Agrippa had Peter thrown into prison when he had James killed. While Peter awaited execution, an angel from heaven caused deep slumber upon the guards and rescued Peter by shattering his chains and opening the prison doors. This account spread amongst all the disciples; thus, despite the persecution, the number of believers, as we called them, continued to grow.

Soon after Peter escaped from prison, Herod Agrippa succumbed to an unexpected demise, and Judea was without a ruler for a time. The emperor, Caligula, too, was stabbed to death; the members of our congregations enjoyed a time of relief from our oppressors even as famine ravaged our land.

It was then that I met him, Saul of Tarsus.

His mission in Jerusalem was the same as mine, to strengthen all our brothers enduring the famine. Barnabas and Titus, a Gentile convert, accompanied him.

These men blessed the brothers in Jerusalem with charity from the gentile congregations that they had established in the northern and western provinces of the Roman empire.

I had not seen Saul since the stoning of Stephen.

He appeared shorter than I recalled. His eyes, no longer as steel, were soft and gleaming. Streaks of grey peeped through his thick, black beard. His robes were without tassels that he had flaunted as a Pharisee. According to his testimony, he considered them as rubbish compared to the knowledge of Christ.

Christ the anointed, the chosen one of God—that is how Saul referred to Jesus. And he preached this *Christ* with unparalleled fervor.

He was in the middle of a speech when I walked into the upper room in the home of John Mark, where the disciples gathered often. I can still hear his words: "We are persecuted but not destroyed; neither death nor life nor anything in all creation will ever separate us from Christ's love; it is this love that compels us, never to rest until his hope lights every corner of the world."

A lump welled up in my throat. Both Saul and James were like thunder. Had James returned from the dead? If only...

I stood spellbound as Saul continued to speak. "Christ is the head of all things, above the universe; in him we live and move and have our being." To our non-Jewish brothers, he was Paul, the name he inherited because of his Roman citizenship. Paul was the beacon of this message: "The Son of God, the Christ, is birthed in us to rescue us from the dominion of darkness and translate us into the kingdom of light."

Barnabas was also bursting with accounts of signs and wonders that the Holy Spirit had manifested amidst the Gentiles. "The sick receive healing, the dead come alive, evil spirits shriek at the name of Jesus."

Barnabas told us of large Roman and Greek cities such as Antioch and Ephesus, where people placed their faith in the risen Christ in droves. Saul and Barnabas had journeyed through the Rome-occupied provinces of Syria, north of Galilee, the island of Cyprus in the Mediterranean Sea, and the northern regions of Lycia and Galatia. Rome's obsession with the construction of roads and highways connecting all its provinces had helped them carry the words of Jesus far and wide.

Saul's words set my heart ablaze. My soul had been in drought after James and my father died. Our nation betrayed us and demanded our blood. How dare they label us as traitors? Anger had clouded love out. Until that day when I heard Saul speak. An undefined force stirred within me. What was it Saul had said? Christ in me? But anger and grief had dimmed the light of Christ. I recalled Jesus' words: "The thief comes only to steal, kill and destroy, but I have come that may have life and have it in abundance."

And to my surprise, during that visit to the famine-stricken land, life welled up in my soul once more. But where was I to go with the message of Jesus?

"The community in Ephesus needs an overseer!" Saul thumped me on the back. His face shone as he spoke.

How did Saul read my mind? Should I go to the second largest city of the Gentiles? Would I dishonor my father's memory if I ate from the same dish as they?

Peter sensed my hesitation and chimed in: "I heard a voice from heaven, 'do not consider unclean that which God has cleansed.'"

A chain fell off my heart.

The next day, I wept as I bid goodbye to my brothers, especially Peter and Andrew. Andrew decided to return to the eastern borders of the empire where he had previously taught. Andrew had never been shy of Gentiles.

I rushed back to Galilee. I sold our share of the fishing business and our home and instructed Mother and James' widow to pack a few things and set off for adventures in an unknown city amidst foreigners.

But before that, I had to take care of an important task.

I dashed to the sea to bid it goodbye. As I stood on the shores, its waves kissed my feet. The waters hugged my ankles in a final embrace. I heard the sea whisper, "It's ok, you can go now."

And I left, never to return.

32

Ephesus, 50 AD

Ephesus, an imperial Greek city, stood in stark contrast to my hometown Bethsaida, a small Jewish fishing village. Even Capernaum, with its great synagogue, was no match for this port city and trade center in the fertile plain of the Cayster River, which emptied into the Aegean Sea. Ephesus boasted in its grand aqueducts and public baths, arches, theaters, gymnasiums, and libraries. Held by one hundred and twenty-seven pillars of marble, the temple of the fertility goddess, Artemis, was the glory of the city whose inhabitants were intensely loyal to their temple, thus not much different from my Jewish fellowmen.

Tall columns lined the public square where the Ephesians loved to gather. Of the three gates bordering the city center, one opened to a colossal library, befitting the citizens who loved to read and debate new ideas and philosophies of such renowned men as Aristotle and Plato. It was to these men and women that Saul brought the message of God's kingdom, the indwelling presence of the divine, who does not require a temple built with human hands. Some accepted his words with an open mind, whereas many ridiculed him. However, the number of those who believed continued to grow because signs and miracles followed him and all of us disciples; many were delivered from sicknesses and evil spirits that held them in bondage.

The community of believers in Ephesus welcomed me with open arms. I bought a small house there to which believers, both Jews and Gentiles, flocked to break bread together and hear the teachings of Jesus. They were in awe: "This man has been with Jesus!"

As time went by, the mingling of Jewish with gentile believers posed a challenge. An earnest debate broke out amongst the leaders of different congregations across the provinces where some of my Jewish brothers demanded the gentile converts practice our laws and customs. Even James, Jesus' brother, favored the demand for gentile converts to be circumcised according to the covenant between our forefather Abraham and God. Saul was indignant. "No man shall be justified before God by works but by faith alone! If we could obtain right standing with God through our laws, then Christ has laid down his life in vain!" It was unbelievable to hear these words from a former Pharisee zealous for the faith of his forefathers, to the point of persecuting those who deviated from it.

But Saul was relentless in advocating for the Gentiles. He summoned a council in Jerusalem where Peter and James, Jesus' brother, who ministered to the congregation there, met with those of us who were ministering to the Gentiles. The council issued a formal degree: "We must not burden the Gentiles with laws whose weight our forefathers could not bear."

I was happy to bear this good news to the believers in Ephesus. Peter, too, ventured out of Jerusalem to minister to the Gentiles. He labored amidst the believers in the city of Antioch, the capital city of the province of Syria, north of Galilee, the third-largest city in the Roman empire. In Antioch, our opposers gave us a new name, Christians, or followers of Christ. A welcome change from being branded as traitors or cult leaders. For we were no longer a mysterious religious cult; we had become a movement, one which continued to gain momentum despite opposition.

Those first few years in Ephesus were challenging. I was glad to have my mother by my side. Aliza proved to be a comfort. She requested training at the gymnasium along with the Greek children and learned to read and write Greek. James would have had a fit, but she knew how to wiggle her way into my heart. I took Greek lessons along with her—me, a pious Jew, learning the teachings and forbidden manners of the Gentiles. Father would turn in his grave, but as for me, there was no turning back.

For in Ephesus, I discovered great freedom.

I had always loved my nation and Jesus more than that. But in Ephesus, for the first time, I learned to overflow with love for those whom my upbringing forbade me from mingling with—those Gentiles with their unclean foods and strange gods.

As this love coursed unhindered through my innermost being, breath returned to my bones. Unbeknownst to me, the load of prejudice had weighed heavily on it.

And the Greeks loved me back. The Holy Spirit, whom they also received, sealed us in this love. They were not as interested in Jesus' teachings as much as they were eager to know him. What was he like? I never tired of describing Jesus' kind eyes, his thoughtful and gentle manner, and his boldness and compassion towards those who opposed him, and they never tired of listening. They loved Jesus without having ever seen him as Jesus had said, "Blessed are they who have not seen and yet believed."

Perhaps it was this love of the people of Ephesus that held me captive there. I resolved to serve in Ephesus till the end.

As Jesus continued to open my heart to his love whose depths were unreachable, I marveled at my ability to scribe these words in my newly learned tongue—Greek: This is love; not that we loved God, but that he loved us and sent his Son as an atoning sacrifice for our sins. Dear friends, since God so loved us, we also ought to love one another. No one has ever seen God; however, if we love one another, God lives in us, and his love is made complete in us. God is love. Whoever lives in love lives in God, and God in them. There is no fear in love. But perfect love drives out fear because fear has to do with punishment. The one who fears is not made perfect in love.

It would take me a lifetime to grow into this love; I would have to withstand the fires of hatred and persecution, that burned against me, and my brothers, for unknown to us, there was trouble brewing in Rome.

33

Jerusalem, 70 AD

Thousands of pilgrims thronged the temple courts to celebrate the Passover, even as legions of Roman soldiers swarmed the holy city. It was not uncommon for Rome to send troops at festivals to uphold order and crush any rebellions that might arise during these mass gatherings. However, this time, thousands of soldiers arrived from Rome with a singular purpose— to subdue Jerusalem for good.

And I was in Jerusalem to fulfill Peter's dying wish.

The last ten years brought sorrow upon sorrow. Andrew's crucifixion was only the beginning. Four years later, the emperor Nero started a fire in Rome, blamed the Christians, and ordered Peter's crucifixion. Paul, who was a Roman citizen, was spared the torture. His death was swift and by the sword.

How did I go on without my brothers? I found comfort in nurturing their legacies, the assemblies of Christians they established throughout the empire. The congregation in Jerusalem that Peter oversaw was foremost in his mind at the time of his death. I resolved to travel to Jerusalem to strengthen those brothers and sisters.

It was my third visit to Jerusalem in the last six years, following Peter's death. It would be my last. As I turned my back on the city of our forefathers, I turned and faced her and wept. I would never see her again; the city which glowed as a bride would soon be downcast as a widow; our temple, the crown of our nation, would be razed to ashes. I fled the city with my brothers and sisters and led them to the safety of the Greek region of Perea beyond the Jordan River.

The demolition of our temple was imminent. The Zealots had gathered all the radicals throughout the Jewish provinces. They protested emperor worship and the draining of the temple treasury by Rome. The Zealots successfully drove out the Roman garrison. Drunk with their newfound victory, they challenged the emperor. The Jewish provinces across the empire banded together and fought in solidarity.

The war against Rome, which began four years prior, showed no signs of dissipating, and Rome experienced a temporary setback when the emperor Nero died by his own hands. The political upheaval that followed worked in favor of my nation, but not for long. During the Passover of 70 A D, the Roman general, Titus, having subdued all radical efforts from Galilee in the North to Judea, arrived in Jerusalem with over eighty thousand men on horses. The daggers of the Zealots were no match for the Roman artillery. The mountain quaked; thuds of heavy stones filled the air as the Romans fired relentlessly upon the city walls, which crumbled to dust.

I, along with the brothers in Jerusalem, escaped in the nick of time. The soldiers sealed the city so none could enter or exit. The siege lasted for over two weeks. Those that did not die by war died of starvation as the Romans seized all supplies and resources. The air was thick with the stench of thousands of corpses, without hope for burial. The Romans stripped the city of every bit of its natural covering. They axed all the trees to build thousands of crucifixes that flooded the land in Jewish blood.

And once again, we Jews were without a homeland. My Jewish brothers scattered, dead or taken slaves. As for the city walls and the temple, not a single stone remained in its place. I recalled Jesus' sorrow as he wept over Jerusalem before his death: "The days will come upon you when your enemies build an embankment against you and encircle you and hem you in on every side. They will dash you to the ground. They will not leave one stone on another."

In an ultimate display of dominion, the Romans set up their banner where the holy sanctuary once stood. Synagogues throughout our provinces, including the one in Capernaum, were razed to the ground as well. Many beat their breasts, saying, "God has cursed us!" But I held on to hope. After all, God did not dwell in temples. Our hearts were to be the holy sanctuary where the Spirit of God lived, and no Roman could ever set up their banner there. What had Jesus said to the woman at Jacob's well? "A time is coming when true worshippers will no longer worship in Gerizim or Jerusalem, but the Father seeks those who worship him in spirit and truth!"

My heart was in turmoil as I lay in bed one night. That day I met with some Jewish brothers who had fled Jerusalem and narrated the horrors of its siege. I had abandoned my Jewish brothers when they fought so fervently for that which I had chased so passionately in my youth—freedom. Moreover, I had befriended some Romans who had joined our congregation of believers. Were they not my brothers too? I had never been one to advocate the sword; however, I couldn't help but wonder if I had betrayed my nation. But could swords made of metal secure our liberty? Jesus' words floated in my mind. "Those who live by the sword will die by it."

Besides, there was another sword that delivered true liberty—the sword of the spirit of truth. It had the power to slay demons, especially those that lurked within. It was this sword which I resolved to bear to all who would open their hearts. For as long as darkness reigned in the hearts and minds of man, there could be no freedom. I grabbed a scroll that night and made this note: For this reason, the son of God was manifest that he might destroy the devil's works.

That night, I was kept from tossing in my bed by another thought which I recorded on the scroll: This is how we know we belong to the truth and how we set our hearts at rest in his presence; even when our hearts accuse us, God, who is greater than our hearts, does not condemn us, for he knows everything.

My heart at ease, I fell into a deep sleep, dreaming of a new day.

34

The Island of Patmos, off the coast of the Aegean Sea, 95-96 AD

I was brought to the island of Patmos in chains by order of the emperor Domitian. The Romans had subdued our nation and destroyed our temple, but to their despair, they could not suppress our message of hope. Many in the empire, both Jews and non-Jews, turned to Jesus and hailed him as the 'Son of God', a title reserved for the emperor. Many acknowledged Jesus as a king whose kingdom was for all people.

Furious that the people swayed towards another king, Domitian enforced emperor worship. He had a temple constructed for himself at Ephesus and mandated sacrifices offered to him, which I opposed. Outraged by my 'treason and audacity', he had me thrown into a cauldron of boiling oil from which I escaped unscathed. This miracle drew more Romans and Greeks to our message, and several members of the imperial household became Christ-followers that day.

Angered and defeated, Domitian condemned me to the island of isolation so I may "preach to the rocks." He instructed that I be granted no mercy.

But who can restrain the mercy of God?

The centurion Flavius Aurelius delivered me to the island. His grandfather was Flavius Marcus, who oversaw Jesus' crucifixion and helped his disciples escape more than once. Aurelius led me to a cave by the seashore at the northern end of the island. He commanded his men to stay on guard outside, and in a stroke of benevolence, he slashed my chains and said, "My grandfather always wished that we may 'deal kindly with the followers of Jesus.' My instructions are to leave you without food or water to be driven insane by solitude and die in your chains. Releasing you from these shackles is all I can do. I trust your God will do the rest. Know that if the report of my kindness reaches Rome, I will pay for it with my head. Therefore, I implore you to hide in this cave until our ship has set sail."

The cave became my shelter for the time of my exile spanning fifty-two Sabbaths. I kept track of the sunsets using seashells to carve lines in the rocks along the barren coastline. I marked each Sabbath with a star.

A large volcano loomed amidst the mountains in the distance. The rocks were my companions by day and my pillow by night. The island vegetation, albeit sparse, broke the monotony of the landscape and provided figs and berries in season.

There was never a dull moment on that island. The birds of the sea befriended me. They flapped their wings and circled over my head, inviting me to join their dance, screaming in glee—the sound of freedom as they soared the skies above the waters. I whirled around with them as much as my feeble frame permitted, a prisoner basking in the sweet delight of freedom.

For no ruler can take captive a heart lightened of its load. At four score and ten years, I had made peace with my demons, especially with my need to rain fire over my enemies. When my demons crept in as shadows, I learned to dispel them with the light of love that Jesus had kindled in my heart. I pitied those beholden to the throne and held captive by its seduction. As for me, I was untethered. And I was home. For once again, I was one with the sea.

The fishes of the Aegean Sea were audacious, unlike the ones in the Sea of Galilee because the waters off the coast of Patmos were undisturbed by boats, except for the occasional Roman ships that delivered prisoners to work the mines at the southern end of the island. The fish swam close to the surface, and I marveled I was still adept at catching them with my bare hands.

The sea threw open the floodgates of memories—my brothers and I pulling our boats out into the water, casting and mending our nets. It was by the Sea of Galilee that Jesus called us to follow him. Zealous for my nation, at barely twenty- three years of age, I left my fishing net to join the Messiah's army to fight beside him, not with a metal sword but with fire from heaven. But Jesus handed me another sword—the sword of truth. Jesus was the fullness of God manifested in the flesh to destroy the works of darkness to set free those bound by sickness, guilt, shame, fear, and a host of inner demons. The fire from heaven that fell on us emboldened us to bear the message of freedom to all peoples, to release each one from their demons. We became enemies of Rome and outcasts at home. My brothers paid for it with their lives. I alone survived. I could have never imagined my life without my brothers, and yet, I had lived long without them; however, there on that island, the bounds of time dissolved. My brothers whispered my name on the breeze that blew inland from the sea. They walked by my side. So did Jesus.

And I saw him once again by the sea.

~

It was the dawn after the Sabbath. I sat by the sea, my feet firmly planted in the sand, the waves crashing about me. I saw him first as a morning mist, then as a pillar of cloud. At first, I perceived it as a fault in my eyes, which had grown dim. They had served me long and well, witnessed both endless horrors and limitless wonders. They had dreamed without ceasing. But that was no dream.

The pillar of cloud assumed the shape of a man, one who walked on water advancing towards me. At once, I perceived it was Jesus. I was caught up in his spirit, which appeared as a mighty wind. Jesus stood before me, not as a mere man, but as the glorious Son of God, the Christ who was supreme above the universe. His hair was woolly and white as snow, his feet as burnished bronze, and his eyes as flame. Light poured from his face. I fell on my knees and buried my face in my hands.

"Do not fear!" His voice put me at ease.

Jesus continued to speak, revealing vivid visions of the secrets of heaven and earth. He unveiled events yet to come. He asked me to write about what I saw and heard.

Pressing on Jesus' heart were words of affirmation and warning for the seven large congregations of Christians in the province of Asia Minor. It had been only sixty-three years since Jesus' ascension to heaven, but his message weathered many storms. Some denied that he suffered in the flesh. How outrageous! I should know. I was there when his veins emptied themselves of the last drop of his blood. How can I ever forget his gut-wrenching scream when they pierced him?

Others found it too good to be true that faith alone should please God, and they added a bunch of commandments and rituals to the requirements for being right with God. These enemies of freedom crept into our gatherings and confused the brothers. Some sought to model the structure of these believing communities after the power structure of this world, once again endangering the freedom Jesus desired for us. His greatest desire, however, was that they remain in his love.

I had nothing to write with, so I used stones to carve his instructions on the rocks. I committed much of it to memory, confident that I would return to Ephesus at an appointed time and transfer Jesus' words onto parchments and distribute them throughout the cities of Asia Minor.

~

Just as a Roman vessel brought me to the island, another arrived to take me home. It was the day after the fifty-second Sabbath on that island. Flavius Aurelius beamed as he alighted the ship. "Your face glows with youth. Your God has been kind to you. Domitian is dead, and the emperor Nerva seeks to release all who are prisoners on account of the message of Jesus. You are going home today!"

I smiled and nodded. "The sea is my home, but indeed it is time to return to the city, for I have much work to finish there."

I set sail for Ephesus. There was much that awaited me there. Long before I was banished to the island, some false brothers crept into our gatherings and swayed the believers. They convinced some of the disciples to continue to offer sacrifices of goats and bulls. Earning the presence of God through these rituals posed a threat to the message for which my brothers laid down their lives, for which I, too, had suffered much. We proclaimed the message of hope—the presence of God has been poured freely on all flesh through the Holy Spirit. I was eager to return to Ephesus, prepared to take on these forces which confused and twisted our message of freedom and put the seekers of God back into bondage.

I vowed to fight for their freedom till my dying breath.

35

Ephesus, 98 AD
Aliza

Uncle John was in the courtyard, sprawled on his favorite wooden chair. The intricate carvings on the chair were his handiwork, a skill he learned from his teacher, Jesus. Uncle John lay still, his cloak snug around his lean frame, his gaze fixed towards heaven—his daily practice since returning from the island of Patmos. He would lose himself in the world of visions and dreams. Upon waking from these trances, he would scribe furiously upon parchments, vivid descriptions of future events, of angels blowing trumpets, of wars and peace, of famines and abundance. He spoke of a new earth.

And a new Jesus. Not one rejected by men, but a ruler over them; a king, riding on a white horse, brandishing a sword made of light, the champion of a new dawn. Anyone may have discounted my uncle's visions as the result of a faltering, aging mind, but I knew better. The miracles I witnessed in his life were proof enough.

The wind was biting, the embers from the fire had died down. Uncle John had fallen asleep with a pen in his right hand and the parchments strewn across the courtyard. His writings were invaluable. None must be lost to the wind! I gathered all his writings and secured them under a stone on the bench by his chair. I grabbed a blanket and trod softly towards him. He seemed content as an infant on his mother's breast. I lifted his left hand, which hung by his side, to place it on his chest.

It was stiff. And cold.

My heart sank. I should have seen it coming. Uncle John's visions had gotten frequent lately. He would say, "I see your father, Aliza, and all my brothers with him."

I took a deep breath and let it sink in. Uncle John was where he belonged—with his brothers. I kneeled beside him, clasping his hand, unable to let go.

There is never a good time to lose the one whose love fills our lives, and Uncle John was my life. My memories of my father were hazy. He was killed by Herod's men, fifty-four years ago, shortly before my sixteenth birthday. Grandfather passed away soon after. I was a young childless widow when we moved to Ephesus over forty years ago. I never remarried. Grandmother died ten years after we moved, and mother followed soon after, leaving Uncle John to fill a formidable void in my life. And he did. I lacked nothing, neither in love nor in strength. I went to school and trained in the gym, alongside my male peers in the city of Ephesus. He also devoted himself to studying the culture and tongue of the Greeks, who populated the large city, a gigantic leap from his small town, strict Jewish upbringing. But Uncle John embraced the challenge. He mastered the Greek language with the enthusiasm of a child. He would say, "There are not enough tongues in the world to report the accounts of Jesus."

In due time, he blended in with the people of whom our forefathers would say, "Do not eat from the same dish as them." It crushed him to be considered an outcast by his people, for whom his heart bled till the end. He would weep for Jerusalem's lost glory, but he was hopeful for a new Jerusalem, which God would establish in due time. Every year, Uncle John honored the Passover. He recounted the stories of Moses and the ten plagues with excitement, but it was when he spoke of Jesus as the lamb on the pole who returned from the dead, his soul would light up. He never tired of telling how Jesus had power over the wind and the waves and demon spirits. Jesus enabled my uncle to do many miracles; however, my uncle never made a spectacle of his gifts, using it only to minister to those in need. He would always say to me, "Little child, love is the greatest power of all."

I sent word of Uncle John's passing to Polycarp, through the servant. Uncle John described Polycarp as "a worthy disciple". He would know how best to preserve my uncle's parchment and deliver his final exhortations to the congregants in Ephesus, Smyrna, Pergamon, Thyatira, Sardis, Philadelphia, and Laodicea, the seven churches scattered across the Roman province of Asia Minor.

I scanned the writing on the parchments. The words were blurred through my tears:

"Dear friends, let us love one another, for love comes from God. Everyone who loves has been born of God and knows God. Whoever does not love does not know God, because God is love. This is how God showed his love among us: He sent his one and only Son into the world that we might live through him. God did not send Jesus into this world to condemn its inhabitants but to forgive their trespasses, redeem them from the burden of guilt, dwell in their hearts by his Spirit, and make them a friend of God. Dear friends, since God so loved us, we also ought to love one another. No one has ever seen God; but if we love one another, God lives in us, and his love is made complete in us."

I wiped my tears as I gently folded the parchment and secured it with a string. It was hard for me to believe that once upon a time, he was known as a son of thunder, a nickname that Jesus gave him and my father. My father lived up to that name until the end, but not Uncle John. He burned with the message of reconciliation and brotherhood until the day he left us.

As I let go of my uncle's hand, I noticed a parchment caught between his cloak and tunic. This is what he saw shortly before crossing over:

"I see a great multitude that no one can number, from every nation, from all tribes and peoples and languages, standing before the throne of God and before the Lamb of God, Jesus. They are clothed in white robes, with palm branches in their hands and shouting, 'salvation belongs to our God and to the lamb'. In the end, there will be no Jew or Gentile, Greek or Roman. There will be only the bel…"

His writing trailed off. The pen was still in his right hand. I slid it from between his fingers, and I used it to complete that last sentence:

"There will be only the beloved."

I pressed the parchment tight against my chest. I did not doubt what my uncle's final words were meant to be, for Uncle John often said, "I am neither a Jew nor a Greek, neither a ruler nor the oppressed, neither a fisherman nor a disciple or overseer, but of this, I am certain—I am beloved."

Bible References

Bible passages and verses woven throughout the plot and used in dialogue are listed below. The NIV Bible translation was referenced according to the terms of use listed by the International Bible Society (www.biblica.com/terms-of-use/).

Chapter 1: Luke 23:2; John 3:2; Matthew 27:40; Matthew 26:53; John 19:19 and 25-29

Chapter 2: Exodus 12: 1-30; Genesis 4:1-16

Chapter 3: Isaiah 61:1-4

Chapter 5: John 1:19-40

Chapter 6: Matthew 4:18-21; Luke 5:1-11

Chapter 7: John 2:1-12; Luke 4:14-29

Chapter 8: Matthew 9:1–13; Matthew 18:21-22; Mark 2:1–17; Luke 5:17–28

Chapter 9: John 2: 13-23; John 3:1-16

Chapter 10: John 4: 1-42

Chapter 11: Mathew 20:20-28

Chapter 12: Matthew 8:5-13 and 23-27; Luke 7:1-10; Mark 4:35-41

Chapter 13: Matthew 17: 1-11 and 20:25; Mark 9:2-8; Luke 9: 28-36; 1 John 4:18

Chapter 14: John 8; John 9

Chapter 15: John 11

Chapter 16: John 12

Chapter 17: John 13-17

Chapter 18: John 18: 1-14

Chapter 19: John 18: 15-27

Chapter 20: John 18: 28-40; John 19:1-16

Chapter 21: John 19: 17-42; Mark 15: 1-47; Luke 23; Matthew 27

Chapter 22: Matthew 27: 3-4

Chapter 23: Matthew 28: 1-15; Luke 24: 1-49; John 20

Chapter 24: John 21:1-14; Ezekiel 37:27; Jeremiah 32:38; Leviticus 26:12; John 1: 14, 18

Chapter 25: Acts 1; Matthew 28:20; Hebrews 13:5; Mark 13:11; John 14:18; John 16:1-4; 12-15; 33

Chapter 26: Luke 24: 13-32; Exodus 3: 1-4; Acts 2

Chapter 27: Acts 3; Acts 4

Chapter 28: Luke 5:10; Acts 1:8; Isaiah 61:1-4; Matthew 10:8; Hebrews 8:6

Chapter 29: Acts 6: 1-15; Acts 7

Chapter 30: Acts 9:1-19; Acts 22: 6-21; Acts 26:12-18

Chapter 31: Ephesians 4:10; Colossians 1:13, 15-20; Acts 26:18, Galatians 2:21; Acts 10:15

Chapter 32: 1 John 4:10-20; Acts 15: 1-30; Galatians 3:5-12; 24-26; Acts 17:16-29

Chapter 33: 1 John 3:20; Matthew 26:52; John 4:23-24

Chapter 34: Revelation 1:1-20

Chapter 35: Revelation 1:11 and 7:9; 1 John 4:7-12; John 21:25; Galatians 3:28

Other References

1. The NIV Bible Online www.biblegateway.com

2. Keller, Werner. *The Bible as History*. 2nd. Ed., William Morrow and Company, Inc. 1980.

3. *Archaeological Study Bible: An Illustrated Walk Through Biblical history and Culture*, NIV. Zondervan Corporation, 2005

4. http://www.gospel.org.nz/index.php/articles/articles-by-rodney/204-john-on-the-island-of-patmos

5. http://wol.jw.org/en/wol/d/r1/lp-e/2012568

6. https://en.wikipedia.org/wiki/John_the_Apostle

7. https://bible.org/article/josephus%E2%80%99-writings-and-their-relation-new-testament

8. http://www.jewishvoice.org/messianic-education/messianic-vision/fall-feasts-and-the-messiah.html

9. https://www.thattheworldmayknow.com/jewish-feasts

Acknowledgments

Thank you, dad and mom, Satish Kant, and Anita Jindal, for giving me wings when empowering the girl child was against the norm. Mom, thanks for taking me to the library every day. It was a long walk, but you never complained. Dad, thanks for believing in me, always.

Thank you to my husband Ravi and my miracles, Yeshupriya and Joshua. Thank you for being patient with me, for holding the fort while I was behind closed doors, writing. Thank you for never complaining, and forever supporting my projects.

Thank you, Shalini Jindal. I will miss our head-on debates while you went through the manuscript with a fine-tooth comb. Thank you for your honest critique and feedback.

Thank you, Nidhi Nathaniel. Thank you for holding me accountable to heed the voice of my soul as I write. You make my writing shine. This manuscript could not be completed without your labor of love.

Thank you, Suzanne Ballantyne, and Marty Sloditski for your kindred spirit, friendship, and camaraderie. You add light to my soul and spark to my writing. I hope we write and work together for many more years.

Thank you, Dr. Jennifer Lowry, for your mentoring heart, for always inspiring me to go after "words that matter". You exude the love of Jesus, and I remain grateful for the gift of *you*.

Thank you, Karen Newton, for the interior design and layout, for shaping my manuscript into a book.

A heartfelt thanks to all members of my family and communities, to my friends, teachers, and mentors who have witnessed my journey and poured themselves into me. Because of you, I am.

About the Author

Pooja Chilukuri is a Nutritional Therapy Practitioner (NTP), Wellness Educator, and a published author. Pooja is committed to helping individuals balance their nutritional deficiencies and help them cultivate healthy habits with ease to prevent or reduce the damaging effects of unresolved, chronic health challenges. Pooja enjoys teaching wellness workshops for individuals, communities, and corporations. She is the co-founder of Healthy Active Aging programs for individuals over the age of forty, to lower their risk of neurodegenerative diseases like Alzheimer's and Dementia. Pooja›s mission is to empower individuals to take charge of their health without being confused or overwhelmed.

In 2015, Pooja published her memoir, *And Then There Was Jesus,* where she shares her journey of recovering from religion, healing spiritual wounds, and discovering herself. Her other books include faith-based poems and reflections and a *Beginner's Guide to Using Supplements* can be found on http:// bit.ly/PoojaChilukuriAuthor

You can learn more about Pooja at www.poojachilukuri.com

Pooja can be reached at pooja.chilukuri@gmail.com

www.ingramcontent.com/pod-product-compliance
Lightning Source LLC
Chambersburg PA
CBHW061211210726
48294CB00006B/1811